"I have sand inside my swim trunks."

Stephen shifted uncomfortably as he spoke.

"Admit it—the swim was worth a little discomfort," Janet said.

"This discomfort is not minor. If you were inside my swim trunks, you would understand why."

"I wish I was inside your swim trunks—" Janet caught her slip and laughed. "I didn't mean that the way it sounded."

At her words, Stephen forgot the sand in his pants entirely. "Oh? What exactly did you mean?"

Janet took his hand and smiled coquettishly. "Come with me and I'll show you. . . ."

"That, Miss Granville, is an offer *no* man would pass up!"

Glenda Sanders had her bags packed and ready the moment her husband announced he'd won a trip to Barbados. It was their first vacation without their two children, and the first lengthy, elegant holiday they'd enjoyed together. Glenda says it really was a second honeymoon with her very own hero of twenty-one years. And, of course, Barbados was a romance writer's paradise, one Glenda now shares with all her readers in her fourth Temptation, *Island Nights*.

Books by Glenda Sanders

HARLEQUIN TEMPTATION

234–GYPSY
257–DADDY, DARLING
277–THE ALL-AMERICAN MALE

Island Nights

GLENDA SANDERS

Harlequin Books

TORONTO • NEW YORK • LONDON
AMSTERDAM • PARIS • SYDNEY • HAMBURG
STOCKHOLM • ATHENS • TOKYO • MILAN

To Rusty,
who took me to paradise

Published May 1990

ISBN 0-373-25400-8

Printed in U.S.A.

1

DOCTORS WERE LUNATICS, Stephen Dumont decided. Creative lunatics with a bent for coming up with absurd euphemisms. *Some discomfort* was a polite little ditty that should be spelled *p-a i-n*. And *temporary immobility* meant a person's knee was going to be about as flexible as a concrete lamppost.

With a grunt of exertion, Stephen leaned on his cane and lifted himself from the third chair he'd rested in since leaving his personal suite. He took a tentative step. An oath forced its way through lips compressed in determination. A sharp dagger of pain stabbed through Stephen's thigh muscle. And a man accustomed to skiing, skating and bounding through life once again planted the tip of his fancy new cane into the thick wool carpet to brace his next taxing step.

The doctor, his mother, his sisters had all advised him to take it slow, to keep the wheelchair handy for a few days so he could pace his recovery. But after six weeks of being imprisoned in a plaster cast and grounded to that chair, Stephen had wanted it out of his sight. He had demanded it be relegated to the Chalet Dumont storage room from whence it had come, to wait for the next skier unfortunate enough to challenge gravity and lose.

He'd been holding on to an idea for six weeks: once the cast was off his leg, he would get up and walk, instantly restored, as though the accident had never happened. Now the pain drove home the unpalatable truth: his recovery would not be swift, and it might never be complete. One didn't maintain the special grace, the oneness with nature, the skill of a Canadian National Downhill champion, with a stiff leg. With luck, he would be walking without his cane soon. With a lot of luck, he might not have a permanent limp.

With a miracle, he might one day ski half as well as he skied before he tumbled down the mountainside.

Mountainside? he thought bitterly. He hadn't even been granted the dignity of wiping out on a challenging slope. Stephen Dumont, son of Olympic medalist Jean-Pierre Dumont and Canadian National Downhill titleholder in his own right, had been knocked off balance and sent careening down the bunny slope by a fifteen-year-old novice skier.

Krissy Crestwell, in tears, had been apologetic as the paramedics loaded Stephen into the ambulance. She'd even sent him a stuffed bear with a cute little plastic cast on its leg and a note wishing him a speedy recovery.

It had not been speedy. The past six weeks had been the longest of his life. After reading until his eyes rebelled at the printed page and watching television until his mind threatened to atrophy, Stephen had insisted on being allowed to do whatever work he could around the chalet. He'd pulled late-night duty at the registration desk and fretted over paperwork for the Dumontique, the chalet's fashion boutique, and for Ski Dumont, the pro shop.

Instead of feeling useful, however, he had grown increasingly frustrated. The mundane busywork reminded him of all the things he wasn't able to do, and as his normal responsibilities were farmed out to his already overworked family members, Stephen had fallen victim to guilt and depression every bit as debilitating as his physical injuries.

Today was his *E* day—*E* for emancipation—the day he'd been focusing on for six weeks, the day the cast was sawed away and Stephen Dumont got out of that damned chair. Today was supposed to be the day he stood up, walked away and never thought of the accident again. And then he'd stood up, expecting some discomfort in his leg, some temporary immobility of the knee, only to discover that pain racked his every step and his newly emancipated knee refused to bend.

Resignedly he limped the last stretch of his journey to the dining room, and settled into the head chair at the family table. Monday was Family Night at the Chalet Dumont. The combo that usually provided après-ski dance music was off, and the Dumont family filled the void with a lot of nonsense the chalet guests seemed to find just offbeat enough to be endearing.

Thirty-five years ago, a beautiful music student named Marguerite Page had walked into the Chalet Dumont to audition for a job playing piano in the dining room. She not only got the job, she won the heart of the Chalet Dumont's owner, Jean-Pierre Dumont. Photos of their wedding had appeared in newspapers and magazines worldwide. It was the Cinderella story of the fifties—Jean-Pierre Dumont, Olympic champion, entrepreneur and international playboy had decided, at age forty, to marry a woman less than half his age.

Three grown children and two grandchildren later, Marguerite Page Dumont still played piano on Monday nights. Her daughters performed with her. Though seldom accused of possessing more than a mediocre talent, Claire and Brigitte carried a tune respectably and showed some aptitude for stand-up comedy.

The truth was, Stephen thought dourly, his sisters were shameless hams who would stoop to unconscionable lows in front of a captive audience. It amazed Stephen that they would actually stand up and execute some of the vaudevillian musical skits they had dreamed up over the years. It amazed him even more that the tourists loved them.

Family Night at the Chalet Dumont had moved beyond tradition into the realm of institution in the Lake Louise ski region. The dining room was packed on Monday nights, even in the off-season. Many of the locals dropped in for dinner just to see how outlandish the Dumont girls would get. And sometimes, on rare and splendid occasions, old Jean-Pierre actually got up and did some soft-shoe with his daughters. Even in his mid-seventies, he retained the grace of a champion athlete. And he unfailingly bent to kiss his young wife's cheek before leaving the stage.

If Jean-Pierre hadn't been out of town on this particular night, Stephen would have begged out of the Family Night follies and stayed in his suite, nursing his depression. He would probably be doing the rest of the family a favor by staying away, he thought morosely. He was too bleak spirited for the zaniness of Family Night. But Jean-Pierre was away, taking care of a problem that never would have gotten out of hand if Stephen had been taking care of things the way he usually took care of them, and Stephen felt obligated to anchor the family table in his father's absence.

Catching the eye of the waiter, he motioned for the young man to bring a bottle of wine. If he had to sit there and endure his sisters' silliness, marveling at the embarrassing depths to which they would sink in the name of entertainment, a little liquid fortification could hardly be considered an indulgence.

"You look sad, Uncle Stephen."

Stephen looked up at ten-year-old Jennifer, who unself-consciously draped a comforting arm across his shoulders. "I'm just a little tired, Jenny-poo. I'm not used to walking anymore."

Jennifer was wearing her Bavarian dirndl, a certain sign she and her older sister were slated to be drafted into the evening's entertainment at some point. Stephen tweaked her braided pigtail. "What have your mom and Aunt Brigitte cooked up for tonight?"

"It's a surprise," Jenny answered.

"I can hardly wait," Stephen said, his intonation heavy with irony.

"It's—" Jennifer caught herself, grinned a Cheshire cat grin and said, "You'll like it this time, Uncle Stephen. You'll see."

"Now why don't I believe that?" Stephen asked. The prospect of a surprise, in the context of Family Night and his sisters, was positively bone chilling!

"You're very cynical," Jenny said.

"Where did a little girl like you learn a word like cynical?" Stephen asked.

"From Momma. She told Aunt Brigitte that's what you were, and I asked what it meant, and she told me."

"Well, if you're so smart, why don't you tell *me* what it means?"

"You don't know?" Jennifer asked. "It means that you're a grouch. Momma said you've forgotten how to have fun. She says you've lost your sense of humor and you need..." She paused to draw in a deep breath, then smiled enigmatically. "Well, you'll see."

Stephen looked at his niece, at the unconsciously provocative smile that would one day beguile young men, and poked Jennifer in the ribs. "Your mother talks too much. And you, little girl, as much as I love you, are female to the core, aren't you?"

"Of course," Jennifer said, with a cascade of giggles. "I'm a girl, silly."

"Where's your daddy?" Stephen asked. A little masculine companionship would be a blessing.

"He's with Nicole. They're . . . she's getting something ready for the surprise, and Daddy's helping."

"I see," Stephen said, afraid he saw too clearly. His sisters were up to something particularly sinister and probably as embarrassing as hell, and both his nieces and his brother-in-law were in on the caper.

Outnumbered by sisters and nieces, Stephen sometimes yearned for a more rarified male atmosphere, for the fraternal camaraderie, uninfringeable by females, that develops between men. Tonight was one of those times. Too bad his father was out of town. Maybe Claude would be able to pull out of Claire's grasp long enough for a quick drink at the bar after the show.

The houselights were dimming by the time Claude stole into the dining room with his eldest daughter. Nicole, two years older than Jennifer, also was wearing a dirndl and a cat-that-ate-the-canary smile. Stephen nodded greetings, then turned to the stage, morbidly curious about what brand of mischief his sisters were conjuring up.

His mother was at the piano, and his older sister, Claire, was adjusting the main microphone. Brigitte, his younger sister, was setting up a mike at the drums. *Another ominous sign.* Brigitte had no formal training on the drums, but she was capable of producing a lot of noise. She was especially fond of cymbal crashes. Even Claire, the tolerant older sibling, tried to dissuade Brigitte from playing the drums more than a couple of times a year. To reserve her talent, so to speak, for really special events.

As usual, the show opened with a lively piano ditty. Then Claire welcomed everyone to Family Night and introduced her mother and sister to the audience. Stephen listened wearily to the stock comments about the Chalet Dumont being a small family-owned, family-oriented hotel.

"We're all family here at Chalet Dumont," Claire was saying, "and every one of our guests is a special guest."

All hundred rooms and twenty suites full of them, Stephen thought snidely. Just one big happy family. Damn, but his leg ached!

Claire called for a round of applause from those who'd been at Family Night at some time in the past and, getting a hearty response, turned to Brigitte and said, "We've got a higher recidivism rate here than a federal penitentiary."

"Our food's better," Brigitte parried.

A titter of laughter passed through the audience, and Claire continued, "All you repeaters know that we don't stand on ceremony on Family Night. When the Dumont family has something to celebrate, we share it. Sometimes we celebrate holidays, you know, like last month—"

"When we celebrated National Polar Bear Appreciation Week," Brigitte piped in.

Claire paused for the laughter to fade. "Well, as exciting as Polar Bear Appreciation Week was, we have something even more exciting to celebrate tonight."

"Is it National Maple Syrup Day already?"

"No, Brigitte. That's not until March. Seriously, folks, we want to do something really different. Tonight we're having a surprise party." She paused again. "All right, I know what you're thinking. It's a surprise to all of you! So we want you to know what you're celebrating. Those of you familiar with the Chalet Dumont and the Dumont family have probably heard about our brother's unfortunate accident at the beginning of the season."

Suppressing a groan of exasperation, Stephen reached for his wine and quaffed it in a single draft. He'd feared something like this.

Claire continued, "Stephen's been confined to a wheelchair for the past six weeks. That's the bad news. But the good news is that today—" a flourish from the piano, a ruffle and cymbal crash from the drums "—Stephen got rid of his cast. We're going to let him stand up for you now, just to prove he can do it. How about a round of applause?"

The spotlight swung over to his table, compelling Stephen to stand up and take his accolades. His smile tightened as a sharp pain shot through his thigh muscle.

"Now," Claire said, "the doctor told Stephen that he needs to exercise his leg, and the best kind of exercise would be swimming. Can you believe it? I mean, this is Canada, and it's January! Here at the Chalet Dumont, we don't *swim* in water this time of year, we slide over it on skates."

The spotlight moved off Stephen, and he sank back into his chair, grateful for the renewed darkness that masked the beads of perspiration that had formed on his forehead.

Claire was still chattering on. "The closest thing we have to a pool at the Chalet Dumont this time of year are the sunken Jacuzzi tubs in the bridal suites. We talked until we were blue in the face, but Stephen absolutely refused to get married just so he could exercise his leg."

Brigitte took over. "We thought of asking for volunteers to go to the bridal suite with him without benefit of clergy, but we just didn't know how we'd screen the deluge of applicants."

Hardy, har, har, Stephen thought.

"Besides," Claire took the floor again, "Papa nixed the idea."

"He tried a weekend like that once and it almost killed him," Brigitte said.

The crowd responded to the reference to Jean-Pierre's legendary playboy days with a roar of laughter, and Claire had to wait to add, "And he didn't even have a broken leg," which brought an even louder response.

"Since we don't have a pool and we couldn't send Stephen to the bridal suite, we—all of us—decided to send Stephen somewhere where there *is* a pool," Brigitte announced.

"With the mood he's been in, we were tempted to send him where the sun *doesn't* shine," Claire said. "But Stephen is our only brother, and we love him—"

"Even when he has the disposition of a polar bear with hemorrhoids," Brigitte interjected.

"So we decided to send him to where the sun does shine over lots of swimming pools, plus two oceans. Stephen's going to Barbados!"

They broke into song, a rollicking barrelhouse tune,

"Stephen's going on a trip—
Stephen's going on a hol-i-day
He broke a bone,
Now his cast is all gone,
Stephen's off on a hol-i-day."

They repeated the chorus twice then called for a sing-along. Nicole and Jennifer, who had disappeared from the table, reappeared from the kitchen, pushing a dessert cart. A spotlight followed their progress, shining whitely on a cake decorated with a plastic passenger plane resting on an island drawn on the icing.

After half a dozen repetitions of the chorus, Claire brought the sing-along to a halt. Then she and Brigitte launched into a speculative discussion about what Stephen might do to occupy his time in Barbados when he wasn't swimming. This led to another original composition.

"Bimbos in bikinis,
Basting on Barbados beaches,
Tall ones, short ones,
Dark ones, blond ones,
Big eyes—so jolly!
Big boobs—by golly!
Bimbos in bikinis,
Basking on Barbados beaches. . . ."

Bimbos in bikinis! Stephen toyed darkly with the idea that he was not a Dumont at all, but had been left on the chalet steps in a laundry basket. He longed for a stiff Scotch. Instead, he found himself in the spotlight again when the dessert cart reached his table and Nicole presented him with an airplane ticket. There was a thunderous burst of applause.

He mustered a smile as he accepted the ticket and the accompanying hug. Jennifer reached under the cart and produced a stack of farewell presents, which contained everything a man needed for a week on a tropical island: shorts, a surfer swimsuit, a pair of sunglasses, two Chalet Dumont designer T-shirts and a Chalet Dumont beach towel.

The show wound up with a rollicking rendition of "Happy Holiday to You," sung to the tune of "Happy Birthday." The houselights came up. Marguerite would continue playing easy listening piano music until her daughters finished dinner and sang a few old songs.

Claire and Brigitte settled at the family table for dinner while the team of waiters went to work serving cake.

"Well, Stephen," Claire said cheerfully, "how does it feel to be taking off to a tropical paradise at the height of the season?"

"My comment would be unprintable," Stephen replied.

Brigitte cocked her head at Claire and shrugged philosophically. "You said he'd either be wildly enthusiastic or hate the idea. I guess we know what way it went."

"It's insane," Stephen said. "It's the chalet's busiest time of the year. We need every person available to keep this place running smoothly."

"'Smoothly' is the operative word here," Brigitte said. "And you aren't helping things run smoothly. You've been a pain in the . . ." Her eyes cut to her young nieces, and she left the phrase hanging.

"Thank you so much," Stephen said dryly.

"The truth is," Claire cut in, "that ever since your accident, you've gotten grouchier and grouchier. Frankly, you've become a liability instead of an asset."

"But I'm out of that damned cast now."

"And in a couple of weeks, you'll be our wonderful, even-tempered sweetheart of a brother again," Claire soothed. "You need some time now to relax and recoup."

"But it's the height of the season. . . ."

"You're not going to get the rest or recuperation time you need if you're here killing yourself trying to prove that the accident hasn't slowed you down," Claire insisted. "Be honest—you expected to get that cast off and pouf! instant recovery, didn't you?"

Stephen scowled at her, but didn't reply.

"It just doesn't work that way, Stephen. Not even for a Dumont." She took a sip of wine, then continued, "If you insist on staying here trying to pretend you're totally back to normal when you're not, you're only going to hurt yourself."

"Or drive us all crazy while you get more and more frustrated," Brigitte said. "Anyway, the ticket is nonrefundable."

Stephen turned his gaze to his brother-in-law, hoping for an ally. "Do you have anything to say about any of this?"

"You might as well give in graciously," Claude advised. "They've got everything planned to the nth detail."

"We found a resort with seven swimming pools and a shuttle that runs every half hour to the beach," Brigitte said.

Claire reached across the table and squeezed Stephen's forearm. "You're a big, strong man, but you're only human. You hurt yourself. Now you have to heal. Go to Barbados. Enjoy yourself. Give your body a chance to heal."

Stephen looked to his nieces, who'd witnessed this family discussion with uncharacteristic silence. "And what about you two? Do you think I should fly off to Barbados?"

"There are beaches there," Nicole said wistfully. "And it's summer."

Jennifer offered grave advice. "I think you should go, Uncle Stephen, but I don't think you should fool around with bimbos."

BRIGITTE, WHO'D LOST the coin toss had been sent to carry Stephen's bags from his suite to the lobby, took one look at her brother and sniffed in exasperation. "What the hell are you doing in wool pants and a sweater?"

"It's below freezing outside."

"But you're going to a tropical island."

"It's now nine o'clock in the morning. It'll be the middle of the night before I even see Barbados. How hot can it be in the middle of the night?"

"Eighty degrees, year-round. I checked."

"That's positively unnatural," Stephen said. "Anyway, you couldn't really expect me to wear those shorts with the flowers all over them. I'd look like a damned tourist."

"For once in your life, you're supposed to *be* a tourist. You're not going to a ski competition or on a buying trip for the boutique. You're going on a holiday."

"In search of bimbos in bikinis?"

"I think a dozen bimbos in bikinis might be just what you need right now."

"Speaking of things that come in dozens—I found the little gift in the bottom of my shaving kit. Honestly, Brigitte, designer colors?"

"No one said safe sex has to be dull! You're going on vacation. Live a little!"

"That's a fine way for a man's kid sister to talk."

"Kid sister? I'm twenty-eight years old. And hot blood runs in the family. I'm Jean-Pierre Dumont's daughter, you know."

"I think even Papa would be shocked at his baby girl coming up with designer condoms."

"You tell him about them and I'll tell about the time I found you and that cashier from the boutique skinny-dipping in the bridal suite Jacuzzi."

"You had no business in that bridal suite, brat."

"Neither did you," she reminded him, and then picked up his camera bag and suitcase. "Come on. It's almost time for the shuttle."

The entire clan was waiting in the lobby to give him the old Dumont send-off, which was, by definition of anything Dumont, loud and boisterous. Stephen suffered the effusive farewells, then was boosted into the Chalet Dumont van by loving hands.

There were four other passengers—a stylish couple in their mid-thirties and two robust young men who looked as though they might have skipped Monday classes to take an unofficial three-day ski weekend. One of the students asked Stephen about his accident and then gave an animated account of having suffered a similar compound fracture while playing high school football.

Stephen listened with morbid curiosity as the kid peppered the story with humor, bragging tongue-in-cheek about the sympathy his cast elicited from cheerleaders and other nubile young women. Stephen wondered grimly if he would ever be able to talk about his own injury with as much nonchalance.

Claude was driving the van, and since he was supposed to meet an incoming flight later in the afternoon, he stayed at the airport to keep Stephen company before his flight took off. "I'm driving, so I'm limited to soft drinks, but I'll pick up your bar tab for the next hour, *mon frère*."

"Talked me into it," Stephen said. Waiting around airports was on his list of least favorite things in life, and when he was headed on a vacation that wasn't his idea, to limp all over a tropical island, a drink sounded like the answer to a prayer. "Scotch. On the rocks," he told the waitress, and casting a grin first to Claude and then to the waitress, added, "The good stuff, not the bar liquor. My brother-in-law's buying."

The Scotch was mellow and smooth. Stephen managed to down a second drink by the time his flight was called, and he and Claude walked to the entrance to the jetway. Claude handed Stephen the bulky bag with the camera Claire had insisted he take along.

"Need help with your carryon bag, sir?" the stewardess asked.

"Of course not!" Stephen snapped, meeting her solicitude with a quelling scowl.

Pink circles rose in the woman's cheeks. "I didn't mean..."

"I'm sorry," he said. "I just... I don't need any help, that's all."

By the time he'd reached the door to the airplane, bearing the weight of the camera bag on his left shoulder and maneuvering the cane with his right hand, he was out of breath and a thin sheen of perspiration shone on his brow. He plopped into his seat with a sigh of relief and let the steward deal with the camera.

Weak. Stephen Dumont was as weak as a kitten. God, but it was frustrating. Humiliating.

The stewardess closed the hatch, then made a preliminary round through first class, offering drinks. Stephen asked for a Scotch. On the rocks.

2

"DID YOU KNOW that the wingspan of a 747 is longer than the first flight made by the Wright Brothers' plane?"

Janet Granville turned to the man in the seat next to her. He was bald, plump, friendly and smelled like peppermint. He didn't look lecherous. "No," Janet replied. "I didn't realize that."

"Mind-boggling, isn't it?"

"Yes," she said absently. "Especially when you consider that, as far as we've come, we still can't get these marvels of engineering into the air on schedule."

Bald, plump and peppermint laughed. "Good point! Imagine, a snow delay in Miami."

Janet's eyes involuntarily cut to the window. Rows of jets lined up against a long building. Crews loading and unloading luggage. Service vehicles. Men in coveralls wearing headphones. Sun glaring off concrete. Not a flake of snow.

Peppermint chuckled again and explained, "We're waiting on passengers who were late making their connection in Atlanta because of a snow delay at La Guardia."

I'll just bet you're a whiz at Trivial Pursuit, Janet thought. How much longer were they going to *sit* there? The air in the cabin was stale.

"The flight from Atlanta should be landing any minute now. The connecting passengers should be boarding in twenty minutes or so," Peppermint continued.

"Twenty minutes or so," Janet murmured. They'd already been on the plane for half an hour, after boarding forty-five minutes late. She was hot and hungry and feeling claustrophobic in the narrow seat.

"Maybe less, if they can herd them down to the gate faster," Peppermint said, then asked, "This your first time to Barbados?"

Janet nodded.

"Beautiful place," Peppermint said. "We go every year. My daughter's getting married there this trip. That's why I'm traveling alone. The wife went with our daughter and her fiancé to get everything set. The rest of the guests are coming this weekend."

"An island wedding," Janet said, relaxing a bit because Peppermint obviously wasn't coming on to her. "That sounds wildly romantic."

"Oh, it is," Peppermint agreed. "Barbados is a wedding paradise. Weddings and honeymooners everywhere you go. Didn't you know that?"

"No," Janet said. "The brochures didn't say anything about weddings. Just sunshine and beaches."

"You meeting someone there?" Peppermint asked.

"Actually," Janet said, "I was supposed to meet someone here. In Miami. My best friend from Minnesota, where I grew up. She and I were going to catch up on old times."

"What happened?"

"Her engine blew up," Janet said. "She had to decide whether to pay an exorbitant amount to get her old car repaired, or whether to buy a new one. She decided to put what she would have spent on the trip toward a metallic blue sports car with a T-top. Although why she needs a T-top in Minnesota escapes me."

"But you decided to go to Barbados anyway," he said. "Good for you."

Janet nodded and suffered a twinge of guilt. "She wanted me to cash in my ticket and fly up to Minnesota for a visit, but it's been a while since I had a *real* vacation, and the thought of all that snow . . ."

"You made the right choice," Peppermint assured her. "The Bajans are very friendly. You'll feel at home in no time."

"I hope so," Janet said sincerely. It really was unfair of Trudy to expect her to feel guilty for not going to Minnesota in the dead of winter knowing, as Trudy well knew, how Janet felt about snow and why she felt that way. They'd made their Barbados plans together, and it was Trudy who'd backed out at the last minute, leaving Janet stuck with paying full price for single occupancy at the resort.

Same old Trudy, Janet thought, pressing her forehead against the window. Janet loved her like a sister, but Trudy's self-centeredness always annoyed her, and for once Janet had refused to give in to it. This time she wasn't sublimating her own needs to do what was convenient for Trudy. She'd been working hard, and now she wanted to play hard, tropical style—lounging on the beach, flirting outrageously, dancing in the moonlight if the opportunity presented itself. She did not need to go to Minnesota to shiver all the way to the singles night spots Trudy undoubtedly would drag her to.

"Where do you live now?" Peppermint asked.

"Central Florida," Janet said.

Peppermint whistled. "That's quite a change from Minnesota. You got folks there, or what?"

"My mom, and an aunt and uncle. My aunt and uncle were snowbirds for years, and finally retired here full-time, then my mother moved down and I followed."

"I'm from Raleigh. I think I'd miss the seasons if I went any farther south. Don't you miss seeing the leaves turn?"

"Yes. But the mild winters make it all worthwhile."

"You'll love Barbados," Peppermint said, then opened the newspaper he'd brought on board. Janet went back to staring out the window.

At the other end of the Miami airport from where the Barbados-bound jet was sitting like a bird with clipped wings, Stephen limped off the plane that had just arrived from Atlanta. His leg was stiff and sore, and the camera bag draped over his left shoulder felt as though it weighed a few tons at least. He nodded to the uniformed airline personnel waiting at the gate and gave them the number of his connecting flight. "That flight's already boarding at Gate 81," the attendant said, and pointed the way.

Stephen had taken scarcely a dozen plodding steps before he felt a tap on his shoulder. It was a woman, quite attractive, wearing the airline uniform. "Excuse me, sir, but you seem to be having a little trouble. We have a courtesy cart. . . ."

Courtesy cart? Stephen thought. One of those little golf carts that went beeping through the airport carrying children and invalids? No way. "Thanks, but I'll make it just fine," he said.

He had gone only a couple of steps farther before there was another tap on his shoulder, firmer this time. Stephen turned. The woman had gone for reinforcements. Stephen frowned at the fresh-faced young man in uniform trying to look authoritative.

The young man cleared his throat. "We realize you can walk, sir, and we don't want to offend you. But we're under instructions to hurry. We've got a planeload of people who've already been waiting over an hour, and we don't want to delay takeoff one minute longer than absolutely necessary. Now if you'll just cooperate, we'll get you to your gate in no time."

Stephen had two choices. He could get on the cart peaceably, or he could make a scene. Cringing with embarrassment, he climbed aboard the ridiculous beeping cart, between a pregnant woman balancing a toddler in what was left of her lap, and a little boy wearing a large badge identifying him as an unaccompanied minor.

He was still stinging with the humiliation of having ridden on the beeping cart an hour later when dinner was served on the plane. He hadn't eaten much on his previous flights, but he'd managed to down two very smooth Scotches during the snow delay at La Guardia, two more cocktails on the way to Atlanta, another two on the way to Miami. The Scotch he'd requested as soon as they'd lifted off from Miami seemed infinitely more appetizing than warmed-over cordon bleu. He might even have a second for desert.

In the back of the plane, Janet attacked her cordon bleu like a person who'd just been rescued after wandering in the wilderness for five days. It was nearly nine in the evening, and all she'd had to eat that day was the package of peanuts on her earlier flight.

Noticing her enthusiasm, Peppermint said, "You'll enjoy the Bajan food. The specialty is fillet of flying fish."

With her tummy full, Janet curled up under a blanket and took a nap. She was nudged awake by Peppermint just in time to watch the sun set outside the window, an awe-inspiring sight even for one accustomed to Florida's panoramic sunsets.

Stephen, whose seat was on the side of the plane facing east, didn't mind missing the sunset at all; he wasn't even aware of it. He'd taken a double dose of aspirin to try to quell the throbbing in his leg, and now his stomach didn't feel so good. He chugalugged the last of his Scotch, hoping the liquid would settle it down. It didn't. He leaned his head against the back of the seat, closed his eyes and tried to forget his churning stomach and his throbbing leg.

The jet reached Barbados a few minutes before midnight, and the airport itself appeared to be asleep. The currency exchange windows, glass-walled duty-free shops and newsstands were all closed, looking eerily abandoned. Though there were six check stations for immigration, only two were manned, so the international air passengers stepped out of the jetway to join one of two serpentine lines. Bleary-eyed, they shifted impatiently, lamenting the lack of fresh air and rest room facilities, both of which were waiting on the other side of the turnstiles at the immigration check stations.

The heat in the terminal was stifling. Janet felt wilted in her sleeveless blouse and cotton skirt. She was about to rummage in her carryon for a rubber band to gather her hair off her neck when she noticed that the wide wall of shoulder muscle in front of her was draped with wool. Having grown up in Minnesota, she recognized quality cashmere at once. Usually she envied anyone who could afford it. Now she felt only pity for the poor northern tourist who hadn't had sense enough to dress for his destination rather than his departure point. If he didn't have cooler clothes in his suitcase, he'd be doing some shopping by the end of his first full day on the island.

No problem, she thought, shrugging away sympathy. If he could afford cashmere, a new tropical wardrobe probably wouldn't strain his budget beyond repair.

His slacks were wool, too, she noticed, an attractive nubby-textured wool of charcoal gray that blended artfully with the pale gray of the sweater. For a few seconds, Janet allowed her gaze to linger appreciatively on the attractive swell of masculine buttocks outlined by that nubby charcoal wool. Then, interest piqued, she raised her eyes to note and admire the wide expanse of shoulders and, higher still, to the thick chestnut-brown hair curving over the starched collar of the shirt he wore under the sweater. The poor fool probably even had a tie on.

She was just stealing a glance at his left hand to see if he was wearing a wedding band when an incongruous movement surprised her. The man wavered, swayed and caught his balance rather jerkily. It wasn't the type of motion she would have associated with such broad shoulders and firm hips, which seemed indicative of coordination and an active life-style.

His latest position had turned him slightly, and she spied the cane in his right hand. There was no time to speculate on the need for it, however, because as he wavered again, clumsily, she caught sight of his face in profile. The sheer male beauty of it made her breath catch in her throat—until she noticed the sheen of perspiration on his flesh, the pallor of his skin made more pronounced by the flush in his cheeks, his irregular breathing, the blank glaze over what otherwise would have been gorgeous brown eyes.

Soused! she realized, suddenly wearied by the inevitable disillusionment of a veteran of the singles war. She'd long ago given up on princes, but she still held out hope that one or two good-hearted frogs were still hopping around in search of loyal companions. But even the promising frogs turned out to have warts, it seemed. Cashmere—and he was as drunk as a skunk.

She crossed her arms over her waist and let out a sigh. Here she was, on holiday, stuck behind a beautiful man in a slow-moving line, and he turns out to be a loser before she can even strike up a conversation.

The line moved a minuscule distance forward, and Drunk and Handsome staggered forward, leaning heavily on the cane for support, even less steady on his feet than before.

Janet picked up her carryon, took a step and waxed philosophical. Beautiful profile, broad shoulders and great-looking behind aside, he'd have probably turned out to be a jerk if he hadn't turned out to be a drunk. There was a rule about it somewhere. Any single woman between twenty-two and ninety knew about the "jerk" rule. Janet had just conveniently forgotten about it while dreaming of a vacation filled with romance and mystery men.

A few minutes later, Janet began to feel genuine concern for Drunk and Handsome. His steps were getting progressively wobblier, and the spots of color on his pallid cheeks were even more marked. His breathing was rougher than before, and the hair curling round his collar was damp.

Everything in her nature told Janet she should help him. He was, after all, a human being in trouble. And if that wasn't enough, helping tourists in trouble was her business. For nearly three years she'd been helping people with special needs, special problems, through Disney World. And occasionally she helped overdressed tourists adjust their clothing to endure the heat of Florida's famous sunshine.

He was in trouble. Someone should get that sweater off him, loosen his tie.... It was almost a reflex action to help him.

No! she thought, resisting the strong urge to tap him on the shoulder. She was on vacation. She didn't have to play the role of guardian angel to anyone but herself for an entire week. *You can't adopt a sad case fifty feet from the airplane!* she told herself. *You came to relax, to have fun. By yourself or with someone who doesn't need a guardian angel. Give yourself a break. Don't adopt trouble just because he's wearing cashmere and has a great tush.*

The reasons she shouldn't involve herself with this man were myriad. She already knew he was drunk. He might be a pervert. An international criminal. Worse, he might be married. Or divorced, with five bitter ex-wives.

Another possibility occurred to her. What if he was diabetic? Diabetics going into insulin shock appeared to be intoxicated when they were actually in a dangerous medical situation. Traveling, a break in normal routine, a change in eating patterns were all potential contributing factors to insulin imbalance. How many times had she heard that in her first aid briefing? From the beginning she'd thought his inebriated state incongruous with his impeccable grooming. And what if he wasn't diabetic—what if he was simply inebriated? Either way, he was a man in need of help. And she had to find out, just in case. If he was diabetic, it could be a matter of life or death.

He took a step and tottered. The sheen of perspiration gave his flushed face an unhealthy luminescence. She tapped him on the shoulder. "Excuse me...."

He turned glazed eyes on her face, and for an instant she feared, from the way he staggered, that he might pitch forward and collapse on top of her. But he righted himself in the nick of time, grimacing as he channeled his weight to the cane.

Tact was an automatic reflex with Janet. "It's terribly warm in here," she said cheerfully, as though she'd known him for years. "I couldn't help noticing that you've got on a wool sweater, you must be uncomfortable. . . ."

"Hot," he agreed fuzzily.

"Why don't you take that sweater off," she suggested. He kept his glazed stare on her without responding. "But first we've got to get rid of this." She slipped the strap of his camera bag off his shoulder and lowered the leather case gently to the floor.

"Camera," he said. "Couldn't check it."

"It'll be fine right here," Janet assured him. "Right now we've got to get this sweater off you." She grasped the bottom of the garment and peeled it upward, helping him the way she'd helped numerous children. He raised his arms obligingly. *Lord, please don't let a kilo of cocaine come off with it,* she prayed, thinking too late of the possibility he might be a smuggler, and that might account for his failure to take off the sweater on his own.

No cocaine. Just a whiff of very expensive male cologne as she pulled the sweater over his arms. "Now, isn't that better?" she said. "Here, we'll tie the arms around your waist, like so. . . ."

Was there a tactful way to ask if he was diabetic? She decided to look for a medical ID bracelet or necklace. "Here," she said, working the cuff link on his left shirtsleeve. "We'll roll these up."

He was docile, acquiescent, as she rolled the sleeve up to his elbow and repeated the process on his right sleeve.

Two cuff links, gold, with the letter *D* engraved on them. No medical ID bracelet.

"I'm putting your cuff links in your pocket," Janet said, and lifted his left hand and pressed it against the breast pocket so he could feel the cuff links there. "You'll remember, won't you?"

He nodded gravely.

"Are you feeling better?" she asked. "You look more comfortable."

He nodded again, but he was still flushed.

"Why don't you take off that tie so you can open the neck of your shirt?" she suggested. And she'd see if he had a medical necklace. "Want me to help you?"

He gave her a cockeyed grin. "You're nice," he said as she worked the knot of his tie down to the second button of his shirt. Was it her imagination, or did she note a flicker of intelligence penetrating the haze in his eyes?

"It's my job to be nice," she replied automatically. She fumbled with the shirt button, surprised to find herself noticing the scent of his cologne and the roughness of a day's growth of beard against the back of her hand as it grazed the underside of his jaw. His Adam's apple protested the pressure of her fingers by bobbing like a startled bird, which startled her into a full realization of the intimacy of what she was doing.

It was impossible, she decided, to be dispassionate while administering first aid to a man after admiring his tush. She searched very quickly for a chain around his neck, and not finding one, took a couple of steps back, distancing herself from the sheer maleness of him, which was having an unsettling effect on her senses.

"Better now?" she asked, noting with relief that his face was less flushed.

"Better," he repeated. She couldn't tell whether he was answering her or merely parroting what she'd said.

"I'm going to ask you a question now," she told him. "I want you to concentrate, please."

Was there comprehension in that blank stare? "Are you diabetic?" she asked. "Do you have any medical problems that could make you confused like this?"

He laughed, a dumb, discordant little sound.

She thrust her face inches from his. "Are you ill? Concentrate, please. Are you ill?"

"Stomach hurts," he said. "Too many aspirin."

Had he overdosed? "How many?" she asked urgently. "How many did you take."

He held up four fingers. Janet exhaled a sigh of exasperation. Was that all? "Did you drink anything with them?"

"Scotch," he said.

"Oh, for . . ." She left the thought dangling as the line moved forward and he bent down to get his camera bag and nearly stumbled. She caught his arm until he regained his balance and then helped him settle the heavy bag over his shoulder again. He took a couple of steps, leaning on the cane, then stopped and switched the cane to his left hand. He rubbed his right hand over his thigh, just above the knee, and she noted the grimace of pain pinching his face.

"Are you hurt?"

"Minor discomfort," he said. The bitterness in his voice was surprisingly clear, considering the state of his inebriation.

He turned to her again and fixed his eyes on her face. "You're very nice."

"I think we've been over this territory before," she said, trying to dismiss him. She'd done her good deed for the day. His drunken stare was beginning to take on the characteristics of a leer, and it was making her nervous. And more than a little hot under the collar of her own shirt.

The leer grew more penetrating, evaluative. "You're not a bimbo, are you?"

The unexpectedness of it, the peculiar, drunken concentration with which he said it, amused Janet. "No," she said, chuckling softly. She thought it best to ignore him then, but ignoring that glazed leer wasn't easy.

"I'm supposed to find a dozen bimbos in bikinis," he announced.

"Good luck."

"Claire said so."

"Is Claire a bimbo?" *Or is she your wife, sending you off with a joke?*

"Claire's a pain in the ass."

"Oh?"

"So's Brigitte."

"You must lead a very interesting life."

He pulled at the collar of his shirt. "It's hot in here."

Janet tried to imagine how much hotter she'd be in wool pants and a shirt with sleeves bunched around her elbows. She pulled a magazine from her carryon and fanned his face.

"You're very nice," he said.

She rolled her eyes in exasperation. That again? "Yes. I'm a very nice person." *Too bad I'm not a bimbo.*

"It's still hot," he said.

"Here, I've got something else that might help." Janet never went anywhere without her foil-sealed towelettes. She kept them in the pocket of her uniform for bathing small, ice-cream-sticky hands, but she'd used them for all sorts of emergencies—including cooling down Yankee tourists unaccustomed to Southern heat. She dug one out of her purse and opened it.

The astringent scent of witch hazel purified the stale air as she laved Drunk and Handsome's face with the towelette. Drunk and Handsome moved his head from side to side obligingly to accommodate her ministrations. Like a cat tilting its head back to get its neck scratched, she thought. He did everything but purr—and she wasn't so sure that the sensual little growl rising from the back of his throat *wasn't* a purr. Abruptly she withdrew her hand and the towelette and was relieved when the line advanced toward the check station.

They were close enough to the desk to hear the immigration agent talking to the tourist at the station. Janet reached into the zippered pocket of her purse for her birth certificate and put it with her airline ticket.

It would have been second nature for her to help Drunk and Handsome find his documents, but she resisted the urge. She wasn't here for a busman's holiday, and he wasn't in immediate danger of keeling over anymore, so he could fend for himself. Any man with a goal as lofty as finding a dozen bikini-clad bimbos should be able to find his birth certificate easily enough.

Not that easily, it turned out. After a lot of fumbling and a lot of coaxing from the harried immigration agent, he eventually produced a Canadian passport in response to the agent's request. The agent aligned the passport and Drunk and Handsome's ticket on the desk and asked, "Where are you staying on Barbados?"

"Swimming pools," Drunk and Handsome replied.

Janet, an inveterate eavesdropper, grinned at his opacity.

The agent repeated the question. Drunk and Handsome expanded his answer to, "Seven swimming pools."

"The Rockley?" the agent asked, and Drunk and Handsome nodded.

"The Rockley. That's right."

The Rockley. The same resort where Janet was staying. Damn! she thought. What was this—kismet? Karma? A strange tremor of anticipation thrilled through her, chased lethargically by a survival instinct warning her that inebriated men running around Barbados in wool sweaters looking for a dozen bimbos spelled trouble with a capital *T*.

She shrugged her shoulders as though she could shrug away the image of his cocky lopsided grin, the way his wool pants strained over his backside. A Canadian. That explained the cashmere, the nubby wool slacks. It didn't explain why he was soused.

The agent shook his head, wished Drunk and Handsome a pleasant stay on the island and pointed toward the baggage claim area. Drunk and Handsome sauntered away from the check station with an unsteady gait, at odds with the cane in his hand and the awkward camera bag weighting his shoulder. Janet handed her papers to the immigration agent and wondered about the cane, remembering the aspirin he'd taken, the grimace of pain on his face, the way he'd massaged his thigh. It occurred to her that he'd never manage a suitcase *and* that camera bag *and* the cane.

When she left the check station, he was standing in the middle of the room looking very disoriented, as though he couldn't quite remember where he was or what he was doing there. Which he probably couldn't, she thought with a sigh of resignation. What the heck. It was kismet, wasn't it? Or karma. It was the least one human being could do for another. She'd just pretend she was back in the Magic Kingdom, taking care of one more tourist with special needs.

She walked up to him, looped her hand around his elbow and said, "Come on, Canada. The luggage is this way."

3

"SCOUTING FOR BIMBOS?"

Drunk and Handsome's eyes were well hidden behind the dark lenses of some very expensive sunglasses, but from the grimace that passed over the exposed area of his face at the sound of her voice, Janet surmised that Hung Over and Handsome would be a more fitting moniker this morning.

He stared at her unabashedly through the dark lenses before answering, "You *are* real. I had half convinced myself that I'd dreamed you up in my drunken stupor."

"A guardian angel?" Janet asked.

"Of sorts," he said, and spread his arm in invitation. "Please, have a seat. Let me buy you a drink in appreciation for all you did for me. If what memory I have serves me correctly, I might well have woken up in some back alley this morning if not for your help last night."

Janet took the proffered seat. Stephen, with reflexive good manners, stood to pull out the chair for her, then resettled into his own seat and raised his hand to summon a waiter. As the waiter scurried toward the table, he turned back to Janet. "What's your pleasure?"

"Diet cola's fine," Janet replied. "It's a little early in the day for cocktails for me." Involuntarily her eyes settled on the highball glass in front of him, and she wondered if she'd made an error in judgment by taking the initiative in renewing their tentative acquaintance.

Following her gaze to the glass, Stephen read her mind and said, "Tomato juice and some kind of pepper sauce. Strictly virgin. I don't subscribe to the hair-of-the-dog-that-bit-you theory."

"Do you feel as though you've been bitten by a dog?" Janet asked.

Stephen, who'd been sipping from his glass, replaced it on the table with a thunk and said, "My head feels as though it was bitten off, chewed up and spit out again by a junkyard cur with foul breath."

Janet sucked her lips against her teeth to suppress a smile. Trying unsuccessfully to sound sympathetic, she said, "That bad?"

"Worse," he grumbled, irritated by her I-could-have-told-you-as-much smugness. He was rarely in a position to have to explain himself to anyone, and it rankled that he felt the need to do so to a near-stranger. It rankled even more to realize that he had only his own foolishness and intemperance to blame for being put in such an embarrassing, defensive position.

The waiter broke up what threatened to become a strained silence by bringing her cola. Janet picked up the tall glass, grateful for the diversion, and took a swallow. "Are you going to be on Barbados long?" she asked.

"Until Monday."

"You're going to be busy, then. No time to waste. Let's see . . . six days. That works out to two per day."

His eyebrows raised questioningly above his dark glasses.

"Bimbos," she said. "You said you have to find a dozen of them."

He groaned and his shoulders drooped. "Did I really bring up that nonsense?"

"You most definitely did," Janet assured him. "You seemed quite discouraged when you realized that I didn't qualify."

"Thank heaven for small favors," Stephen muttered under his breath.

"You'd probably have better luck bimbo hunting on the beach," Janet suggested, looking around the nearly deserted courtyard. The breakfast crowd had dispersed, and the swimming pool that gleamed brightly in the sunlight was empty.

"I'm not in a bimbo-hunting mood."

"Aw," Janet said. "Claire's going to be so disappointed."

Stephen winced. "I mentioned Claire?"

Janet nodded. "Brigitte, too."

This time he groaned. "My sisters . . . Did I mention that they sing?"

Janet shook her head.

"Another small favor to be thankful for," Stephen said. "I seem to have been in a talkative mood last night."

"You did mention a particular anatomical complaint associated with them."

"Whatever I said, those two deserved every word of it."

"Too bad this isn't Haiti. You might be able to find some voodoo dolls there."

Stephen heaved a sigh and winced at the pain the effort sent shooting through his head. "I'm not sure the situation merits voodoo dolls. Claire and Brigitte mean well, I just . . ." He drew in a breath. "I don't like being bullied."

I just bet you don't, Janet thought, looking at him over the rim of her glass as she took a sip.

"What about you?" he challenged rhetorically. "Do you have brothers that you bully unmercifully under the guise of what's best for them?"

"Sorry," she said, shaking her head. "No brothers at all."

Hung Over and Handsome smiled for the first time. "You wouldn't bully them if you had them, would you? You're too nice."

Ignoring the effect his smile was having on the pit of her stomach and the hairs at her nape, Janet said, "We covered this subject last night."

"Did we get around to introductions?"

"Not exactly. But I had the advantage of seeing your passport as you breezed through immigration, Mr. Dumont."

"And you are?"

"Janet Granville," she said, offering her hand across the table.

He studied her hand a moment before wrapping his own around it in a firm handshake. "Well, Janet Granville, when I was doing all that talking last night, did I happen to thank you for all you did?"

"I believe 'thank you' was the last thing you said before passing out."

"I'd like to say it again, cold sober this time. I woke up in a proper bed and the proper hotel with all my luggage intact. I'm indebted to you for that."

"Just helping out a fellow tourist," Janet demurred.

Stephen surprised her with a cunning grin. "It wasn't you who undressed me, was it?"

"It was the porter who drove the golf cart from room to room when we checked in."

"Did you watch?"

"The porter insisted on a witness. He didn't want to be accused of robbing you blind while you were unconscious. Since I seemed to be in charge of you . . ."

"Uh-huh."

"If I hadn't agreed, you'd have been stuck in those wool pants all night."

"So being the angel of mercy that you are—"

"I rallied my courage and did my humanitarian duty," Janet said. "Oh, and don't worry—I'm the soul of discretion. I won't breathe a word about your baby-blue skivvies."

"Observant little humanitarian, aren't you?"

A yellow bird, hardly as large as a butterfly, swooped down from one of the hanging planters and began scavenging the tabletops for crumbs. Stephen gave the tiny bird an incredulous looking over. "Bold as brass, isn't he?"

"I saw one at breakfast trying to get into the pancake syrup. They tell me they fly right into the bungalows if you leave the windows open."

"Something thrilling to write home about," Stephen said drolly.

"I saw some photo postcards with yellow birds on them in the grocery store," Janet said helpfully. "It's around the corner, near the boutique."

"Give it up, Ms. Granville. I'm here under duress. I plan to send my sisters the ugliest, gaudiest, raunchiest postcards on the island."

Janet rescued her drink from imminent plunder by the yellow bird and drained the last of the cola, then replaced the glass with a thunk of finality that set the bird into flight. She and Stephen followed its course until it perched in a hanging basket of geraniums.

"I've got to be going," Janet said, slipping the strap of her purse over her shoulder.

"Taking a tour?"

"Just engaging in a typical American capitalist activity. I hear the shopping in Bridgetown is world-class. I'm going to go sniff perfumes and test the weight of Baccarat crystal in my hand at the duty-free shops and pretend I'm a wealthy American in search of bargains."

She tossed Stephen a casual grin. "If I find any really awful postcards, I'll leave them at the desk for you."

"At the desk? Not my door?"

"The quality of my mercy would be strained by to-the-door delivery," Janet said. "Besides, you'll probably be too busy on your quest to hang around your bungalow."

"Quest?"

"The dozen bimbos in bikinis," she reminded him. "I should think you'd do your stalking at the beach."

Frowning, Stephen grumbled, "Raunchy postcards are too good for them. I've a good mind to fly home and throttle them."

"Claire and Brigitte?"

"Who else?"

Without thinking, Janet reached across the table to cover his hand. "You'll feel better after you finish your tomato juice. You have taken something for that head, haven't you?"

"Extra strength," he said. Abruptly he closed his hand around hers. "You really are nice, aren't you?"

Janet laughed softly. "I'm getting a keen sense of déjà vu." She stood up, gently retrieving her hand. "I'll keep my eyes open for raunchy cards."

Stephen watched her walk away, taking advantage of the first opportunity he'd had to get a good look at the full length of her. Her figure didn't have a show-stopping perfection but, like her face, it bore up well under close scrutiny.

Cold sober, Stephen had found Janet's face intriguing. He found her figure voluptuous. The shorts she wore allowed him a generous view of her legs. While they didn't have a fashion model's svelte length, they passed muster. He observed her closely, noting details of her movement—the slight sway of her full hips, the sureness of her step, the way her dark hair bounced teasingly over the tops of her shoulders. Even in dim light and from a great distance, her body would be readily identified as female.

He watched until she turned a corner that took her out of his view, then, without the distraction she provided, became freshly aware of his aching head. It was damnably hot, too, and inside his heavily starched cotton pants, his incision was beginning to itch almost as much as it had inside that despicable cast. Even his tomato juice had lost its chill and tasted medicinal. Suddenly repulsed by the smell of the pepper sauce in it, he slid the glass to the center of the table.

He propped his elbow on the table and his chin on his balled fist and sighed his frustration. It occurred to him that the few minutes just spent in the company of Ms. Janet Granville might possibly be the one bright spot in the entire week of this forced vacation. She was quite a package, his Good Samaritan. Too bad he'd been soused when he met her, unconscious when he'd been undressed in front of her and hung over when he'd expressed his gratitude for her mercy. Just thinking of the impression she must have of him made his head ache all the more.

The yellow bird flew down and lit on the edge of his glass, then dipped his bill to drink.

"You're going to be sorely disappointed, *mon ami*," Stephen predicted, but the bird persisted. Then, tasting the sting of the pepper sauce, he cocked his head at Stephen and gave a chirp of protest. Stephen shrugged his shoulders. "I tried to tell you, no?"

Stephen felt a peculiar kinship with the bird; at the moment, he was not finding the taste of life particularly sweet, either. In addition to his physical discomforts, he found himself victim of an emotional malaise, as well, a vague restlessness that came from having been wrested from his normal routine and environment. Accustomed to a heavy load of responsibility that kept him constantly busy, he found the sudden freedom and idleness disconcerting. Used to being surrounded by family and the extended family of guests at the Chalet Dumont, he felt isolated and alone.

For a few minutes, Janet Granville had breached that sense of isolation; now she was gone.

He signaled for the waiter and ordered a lunch of assorted fruits and cheeses. The restlessness lingered, but the protein in the cheese eased the ache in his head somewhat, leaving him free to ponder the predicament into which he'd been thrust by his well-meaning loved ones.

He reached the only conclusion a logical mind could reach and decided to act in the only reasonable way possible. He was stuck on this tropical paradise for a week, whether he liked it or not, so he might as well make an effort to enjoy himself. If he didn't have a good time, he should at least have a less miserable one.

An inquiry at the registration desk led him to an attractive black woman who presided over a desk at the far side of the lobby. After introducing herself as Regina, she bade Stephen to sit in a chair facing the desk.

"So," she said, "you want to know what to do on de island. Our coast is lovely, anytime. Dere you go sand side, to de beach. And you take a sea bath. A swim. We have shuttles leaving every half hour."

"I'm not crazy about the beach," Stephen said.

"Tonight at eight, de Rockley has its weekly Bajan buffet wid fashion show and entertainment. No reservations required."

"That sounds promising," Stephen said politely.

If Regina noticed his lack of enthusiasm, she showed no sign of it. "What else are you interested in? Tours? Entertainment? Sports? De scuba diving is excellent, and parasailing . . ."

Stephen dropped a disgusted glare at his leg, which was still stiff, itchy and achy. "I'm afraid sports are out on this trip."

Regina opened a scrapbook and turned it so he could see a colorful plastic-clad brochure. "De *Jolly Roger* has day and night cruises. De fee includes transportation, food, all de pirate punch you can drink and a pirate wedding. And you go jump up. Dancing."

A perfect opportunity for bimbo hunting, Stephen thought, studying the photo of the mock pirate ship, its decks packed with partying adults in swimsuits. Still, the idea of trying to balance on his sore leg on a pitching ship took all the fun out of the prospect of stalking bikini-clad women. "I don't think so."

Undaunted, Regina said, "If you're interested in Bajan history and culture, you won't want to miss *1627 and All That*. It's a musical revue wid native dances at de Barbados Museum. The price includes admission to de museum before de show and a Bajan buffet. T'ere's a performance tomorrow night."

A musical revue certainly held more promise than trying to balance on a rocking boat. "That sounds fine," he said. "How do I make reservations?"

"I can make dem for you."

He nodded acquiescence. "Now what about tours?"

"Basically, t'ere are two types. One is an eighty-mile bus circle of de island, and de other is a beach walk dat ends wid a party—rum punch included." She flashed a smile. "Do you want to see de sights, or do you want to drink rum punch and do de limbo? It's your vacation."

Stephen unconsciously wiped his open hand against the thigh of his injured leg. "I'm not up to much walking," he said. "Maybe the bus tour."

"It's an all-day tour. Do you want to try for Friday?"

"Yes. Let's do that."

He waited while she made the calls, then gave him reservation numbers and the specifics of when and where to wait for the buses. "Is t'ere anyt'ing else I do for you?" she asked.

"Not unless you can lower the temperature a bit. Perhaps five degrees."

She laughed. "Dat I cannot help you wid. You'll have to go Bajan, Mr. Dumont. Shorts or beachcombers would be much more comfortable dan dose heavy pants. Near de beach, t'ere are many shops with colorful beachwear. And dere's always Bridgetown. You can find anyt'ing you need dere."

Bridgetown. Where Janet Granville was immersing herself in the decadent splendor of designer perfumes and Baccarat crystal with capitalist abandon. The thought brought the first genuine smile of the day to his lips.

"How do I get to Bridgetown?" he asked.

"T'ere's a bus stop near de entrance to de resort. But if you don't want to do so much walking, you might be better off wid a cab dat will take you into de middle of de shopping district."

One taxi ride and a short stroll later, Stephen was in the middle of a department store called Cave Shepherd. Though the thought of having anyone seeing his cast-bleached leg with its ugly surgical scar was repugnant, so was the prospect of spending a week with his incision site damp and itching inside a cotton steam cabinet.

He found the men's department easily enough and soon was sifting through a rack of cotton shorts, looking for anything in his size that didn't have bright flowers on it. He found two pairs, one khaki and the other white, and carried them to the cashier.

He was one person away from the register when he spotted Janet Granville riding the escalator from the level above, carrying several plastic shopping bags. If there had been any doubt in his mind as to the real reason he'd made the jaunt into Bridgetown, it evaporated as relief poured through him at the sight of her. He watched closely as she stepped off the escalator and followed the main aisle to the perfume counter, where she picked up a bottle and read the label.

Still clutching the shorts he'd picked out, he slipped behind her. "Finding any irresistible bargains?"

Startled, she jerked round to face him. "Stephen?" she said, and when she'd overcome her shock, added, "Hello." Her face broke into a wide smile.

"I see you're giving Barbados's economy a shot in the arm," he said, smiling as he motioned to her shopping bags.

"I just noticed this perfume, called Khus Khus. I just bought some sachets made from *khus khus* root in a small shop down the street. It's a grass that has a pungent aroma. They weave the roots into hangings for closets and such to freshen them. I think they add spices, too."

She held up the bottle. "When I saw the name on a fancy bottle, I had to investigate. This is made in Jamaica, and packaged as a designer fragrance. Sort of a Caribbean essence. Interesting marketing approach, isn't it?"

"Quite clever," Stephen said, thinking how well something similar with a "ski" scent would sell in Dumontique at the chalet.

"What about you?" Janet asked. "Are you buying those?"

Stephen nodded self-consciously. "I'm going native."

"That's a very sensible move. You could suffocate in Canadian clothes in a tropical climate like this."

"Either you've been here before, or you did your homework well," he said, eyeing her from head to toe and thoroughly appreciating the parts of her left uncovered by her shorts and shirt. "You've already gone native."

"I *am* native," she said, laughing softly, then explained. "Not to Barbados, of course, but I live in Florida."

"Florida?" he repeated, surprised.

"Yes. Florida. You know—beautiful beaches, retirement communities, Cape Canaveral, Disney World. The climate's not quite as consistent as it is here, but it's similar."

"Then what are you doing here? This must be just like home to you."

"It's a long story," Janet said. "But the bottom line is that I *hate* snow!"

"Hate snow?" Stephen said incredulously. The very idea was too preposterous for a dedicated skier to contemplate. "How could anyone hate snow?"

"Oh, it's easy when you've been in enough of it," Janet assured him. "What about you? Isn't that why you're here—running away from the Canadian winter?"

"I'm here," he said, gritting the words through his teeth, "because Claire and Brigitte publicly humiliated me, then bamboozled me into getting on the plane."

"So you could find a dozen bimbos in bikinis?"

"Yes. Brigitte even—" He stopped short of mentioning Brigitte's parting gift, which, in a perverted way he supposed, showed a certain measure of concern for his general health and welfare.

"Even?" Janet prompted.

Stephen exhaled a sigh of one sorely oppressed and said, "You don't want to know."

"We're going to have to swap stories," Janet said. "Mine's long, but I have a feeling yours is a lot more interesting."

"Let me pay for these and we'll find a place to sit down, maybe have a cup of coffee?"

"I saw a deli upstairs," Janet said.

Since she'd eaten a big breakfast with an eye on skipping lunch to economize, Janet opted for gourmet ice cream instead of coffee. She let the first spoonful of pistachio nut melt over her tongue and sighed with obvious relish.

"Good?" Stephen asked.

"Heavenly."

Stephen found that amusing. "So tell me how a woman can love ice cream and hate snow."

"They're totally unrelated," she said. "There's no connection at all. Ice cream is a sensual delight, and snow is—" She sucked in a breath. "Snow is terrifying."

Stephen found himself resisting a strong urge to dash around the table and take her into his arms when she succumbed to a tremor of pure emotion. The terror she spoke of was close to the surface. "You had a bad experience?"

"Lots of them, actually," she said. "I grew up in Minnesota, and I guess you could say snow was always a nemesis. Most of the experiences were just inconveniences—being snowed in on special occasions, having to cancel plans, that kind of thing. I was supposed to have a slumber party on my eleventh birthday, but it snowed and no one could get there."

Stephen thought about his niece Jennifer and how she faced life's little disappointments. "You were heartbroken."

Janet squared her shoulders. "I got over it. We lived in Minnesota. Blizzards were a part of life. It wasn't until years later that I realized the real antipathy I felt for snow. Actually it had never even occurred to me that I had a choice, until my aunt and uncle started flying south for the winter and came home every April with suntans that made the rest of us look like pickled eggs in comparison."

She took another spoonful of ice cream and let it melt in her mouth before swallowing.

"So you decided to move to Florida so you wouldn't look like a pickled egg," Stephen said. The way his eyes caressed her face told her he didn't think she resembled a pickled egg in the least.

"It wasn't quite that simple. My aunt and uncle decided to stay in Florida year-round, and then my father died unexpectedly, and my mother spent a winter with them and decided to give it a try."

"You went with her?"

"Only for a visit, at first. I'd lucked into a very good job—or what I thought was a very good job—after college, and I wasn't sure I wanted to leave it. And there was a man I was dating, and several good friends. One in particular—Trudy. We've been friends since grade school, and we had a darling apartment. We'd decorated it ourselves, just the way we wanted it. We felt so grown-up and independent."

"Except that you turned into pickled eggs in the winter," Stephen teased.

Janet was not amused. "Except that she came down with the flu one January. She'd called in sick that morning, and when I got home from work that afternoon, she was running a high fever. That was when I realized we didn't have a can of soup in the cupboard or a chicken in the freezer. No orange juice—nothing for fighting off the flu."

Again she sucked in a shuddering breath, as though fortifying herself against a very unpleasant memory. "I knew it was going to storm, but I thought I could get to the store and back before things really got bad. I didn't even bother with the tire chains, because I thought they would take too much time and slow me down."

She took another spoonful of her ice cream, and Stephen sensed how loathe she was to continue with the story. He was considering a tactful way to let her know she didn't have to go on, when she said abruptly, "I made it halfway home before my car slid off the road into a drift."

She paused again, staring at the mounds of ice cream seeping into puddles in her dish. "It was eighteen hours before they found me. I wasn't sure they'd find me at all. I had a blanket in the car, but I hadn't even worn my heaviest coat. I had to put the cheese and the cans of soup I'd brought inside my clothes to keep them from freezing, in case I needed them. And I was frantic about

Trudy, worried that she'd get critically ill with no one to take care of her and nothing to eat or drink."

Her eyes locked with Stephen's. "By the time they found me, I'd sworn that if I got out of that car alive, I'd go somewhere where I'd never be cold, ever again, or see another flake of snow. And I did. That's why when Trudy and I decided to go on vacation together, we chose Barbados."

"She survived the flu, obviously."

"Trudy survives everything," Janet said wryly. "She's like a cat, she lands on her feet every time. While I was trapped in a snowdrift, worrying myself silly about her and almost freezing to death, she was being nursed by the neighbor across the hall who had fortuitously dropped by to ask if we had any candles in case the electricity went out in the blizzard. He was gorgeous, of course, and he'd been a medic in the army. He was there to hold her hand after she found the presence of mind to worry about me."

"She's joining you here?"

Janet frowned. "That's another Trudy story. Her car blew up, so she took her vacation money for the down payment on a better one and canceled out last week. She wanted me to come visit her in Minnesota, but I said, 'No, thanks.'"

Smiling unexpectedly, she said, "So, now you know how I came to be in Barbados. What about you?"

He told her about Chalet Dumont, his ignominious spill down the mountain, his frustration in the wheelchair, his sisters' brainstorm about sending him on a holiday, their performance on Family Night.

"So there they were," he concluded, "singing about bimbos in bikinis while I slowly died of embarrassment, and the next thing I knew, I was on an airplane."

"Your sisters sound delightful."

"Wily as coyotes," Stephen said. "And as tenacious as a virus. And raising my nieces to be just as sneaky."

Janet couldn't keep from smiling at his tough-guy act, when his affection for his family was obvious in every grumbled syllable. After a comfortable lull in the conversation, she said, "Does your leg still hurt?"

He shrugged. "I can live with it."

"The way you lived with it on the plane last night? With aspirin and Scotch whiskey?"

Groaning, he said, "Don't remind me of that foolishness. My head still hasn't recovered."

An awkward silence ensued before he said, "Last night was . . . it was inexcusable, and really not typical. I just kept getting on airplanes, and my leg was hurting, and I kept ordering drinks, and then they put me on that ridiculous cart, and . . ."

He waited for her to respond. When she didn't, he said, "You believe me, don't you?"

"What ridiculous cart?" she said, enchanted by the vulnerability at odds with his rough, tough demeanor.

"You know, one of those stupid carts. The kind they put kids and invalids on."

"When did they put you on a cart?"

"In Miami. Our plane was late getting in. I wasn't too steady on my feet, and I guess they thought it would be quicker for me to ride. So I got on with a pregnant woman and a little boy with a sign around his neck, and the damned cart went scooting through the airport going beep, beep, bee-e-ep."

Janet giggled softly at the incongruity of the virile male in front of her being subjected to such treatment. His speech was accented by a mild trace of French that made his account of the ordeal all the more charming.

Indignant in the face of her amusement, he said, "It was almost as humiliating as having Claire and Brigitte singing about my wandering over Barbados in search of bimbos in bikinis."

"Poor baby," Janet said, swallowing the urge to giggle.

The droll expression of sympathy held sincerity and was as soothing as a hug to Stephen's wounded body and battered ego.

"Do you have more shopping to do?" he asked after finishing his coffee and replacing his cup with an air of finality.

"No." She smiled impishly. "But I saw some postcards you might be interested in. Want me to show you the shop? Unless you have more shopping—"

"I don't, and I do," he said, then clarified, "have shopping to do and want to see the postcards. Shall we go?"

4

THE SHOP WITH THE POSTCARDS was sandwiched between a dress boutique and a jewelry store in a mall several blocks from Cave Shepherd. The store itself was scarcely five feet wide, but was deep, and every inch on its long side walls was covered with paper—postcards, informal notepads, fine deckle-edge stationary.

Just as the quality and function of the stock was varied, so was the wide range of art decorating the paper products. The postcards featured everything from full-color photographic reproductions of world masterpieces to cartoon treatments of island scenes to bizarre photographs.

"What do you think about this one?" Stephen asked, after browsing through the novelty postcards.

Janet studied the card he was holding. A flying fish, Barbados's trademark native food, had been drawn to resemble a jet aircraft with the marking, "Gourmet Bajan" on the side. It had been given a face with exaggerated features and was ludicrous through sheer ugliness.

"If I ever found anything remotely resembling that on a plate, I'd cut my vacation short and head home!" she replied.

"Good," Stephen said. "I'll get it for Claire. Brigitte gets the limbo dancer."

"Are you *sure* you want to send that limbo dancer through the international mails?" Janet asked.

The limbo dancer, a robust man, had been photographed from a camera stationed on the ground in front of him, and the peculiar angle emphasized the bulge straining against the crotch seam of his pants. Janet had been embarrassed when she'd spied it earlier while shopping alone; she'd blushed when Stephen had pointed it out as a possible choice for his sister.

"Oh, yes," Stephen said, teeth gritted. "It serves her right for—" He cleared his throat self-consciously, thinking of Brigitte's little departure gift. "It's just what she deserves."

"I'll bet you used to throw spiders at your sisters when you were younger."

"I never did such a thing!" Stephen said, offended by the unfair accusation. "I was always nice to them, and they used to gang up on me. . . ."

"Totally without provocation, of course."

"Then run screaming to Maman if I gave them so much as an ugly look. Claire was always bossy, and Brigitte was a brat from the day she was born."

"It must have been horrible for you," Janet said.

Stephen ignored her droll irony. "I used to dream of having a brother who didn't giggle over silly things and squeal when he saw bugs and cry over dumb things."

"To even the odds," Janet suggested. "So they couldn't gang up on you?"

Stephen frowned. "Yes."

"Poor baby," she said. "Being sent off to a vacation paradise against your will. Forced into a land of sunshine and turquoise beaches."

"Heaven help me if you ever meet my sisters and join forces with them. I could end up on the first public shuttle to the moon."

"It sounds as though they care a great deal about you."

He laughed diabolically. "And I care a great deal about them. I'm sending them postcards, no?"

Janet groaned softly in exasperation. "Such thoughtfulness could get you nominated for Brother of the Year."

He paid for the cards and they left the shop, window shopping in the small mall on their way to the door that led to the street. Outside, they stopped to get oriented.

"The taxi stand's in the next block," Stephen said, after getting his bearings. "Ready to go back to the hotel?"

"Yes, but . . ." Stephen raised his eyebrow inquisitively, and she explained, "It seems silly to pay for a cab, when the bus stops right at the Rockley."

He could have given her a list of reasons to opt for the taxi, topped by comfort and convenience. But before he could, she challenged, "What's the good of traveling if you don't get out and mix with the natives?"

To that, he had no immediate reply.

"Come on," she said, grabbing his arm just above the elbow and leading him in the opposite direction from the taxi stand. "I rode it into town and it was great fun. The driver was playing calypso rock. Don't you want to see what the *real* Bajans wear and eavesdrop on conversations?"

"Eavesdrop?" Stephen fell into step beside her, trying to ignore the shooting pains stabbing through the dull, steady ache in his injured leg. "I wouldn't have believed it of a nice person like you."

"It's not a sinister type of eavesdropping," Janet said. "It's a way of communing with the people, finding out what they're thinking. What they're worried about. What excites them. What their passions are."

"I see."

Janet paused in midstride to look up at him skeptically. "Do you?"

"It's easy to see what your passion is."

"*My* passion?"

Haphazardly looping his shopping bag on the handle of his cane so he'd have a free hand, he caressed her cheek with his fingertips and said, "People, of course. I'll bet you collect them the way some kids collect stray kittens and puppies."

His fingers were warm on her skin. "No, I—"

"You collected me," he said. "No one else came rushing to my rescue."

"I thought you were going into diabetic coma," she said, twisting her face away from his hand as she resumed walking.

Stephen hastily reshuffled his shopping bag and cane and hurried to catch up with her. He muttered a curse and grimaced as a pain shot up his thigh, but Janet didn't hear.

She stopped abruptly and snapped, "It's not a crime for a person to care about her fellow human beings."

"I never said it was." He winced as he halted beside her just as abruptly.

"Is your leg hurting?"

Stephen's lips momentarily hardened into a frown, then relaxed as he exhaled heavily. "I took aspirin before I left the Rockley. I guess they're wearing off."

Janet reached into her purse and began rummaging. "I have some with me. We can get you something to wash it down with at one of the vendor carts."

He grinned at her as she offered him the purse-sized tube. "If I needed a cough drop, I'll bet you could produce it."

"If you *desperately* needed a cough drop," she said tersely, "I'd offer to go to the pharmacy I saw this afternoon."

He dropped a kiss onto her forehead, then gave her a fetching smile. "You're sweet, Ms. Granville."

"Sweet?" Janet said. "*Sweet?*"

"As a sugar cookie," he assured her, then nodded toward the row of cart vendors in the next block. "Come on. Let's see what they've got to drink."

"I don't think I like being 'as sweet as a sugar cookie.'"

"Don't go getting offended," Stephen said. "Being sweet is no disgrace. I was complimenting you."

"I think I'd rather be a bimbo than a sugar cookie."

"Does that mean I'll get to see you in a bikini?"

They'd reached the row of sidewalk stalls. Passing up the fresh fruits offered by the vendors, who stood poised to open fresh coconuts or dice pineapples with long, menacing knives, they found an elderly black woman selling colas and bottled fruit juice from a pushcart. A broad smile deepened the laugh and squint lines on her sun-wizened face as Stephen counted Bajan dollars into her hand to pay for the drinks, and she laughed aloud when Stephen insisted she keep the change due him.

"T'anks, mon," she said, tucking the bills into her pocket. "You havin' a good, good time on de island, 'ey?"

"We'll do that," Stephen said, casting Janet an amused sidelong glance.

"You jump up de limbo?" the woman said, leaning back and gyrating her hips with surprising dexterity.

"No limbo for me this trip," Stephen said, bobbing his head toward his cane.

The woman shrugged and tapped the back of her hand against his chest conspiratorially. "You just be limin' den, mon."

"Limin'?" Stephen asked.

"Limin'," the woman snapped back as though she couldn't believe he'd had to ask for an explanation.

"Takin' t'ings easy, mon. Standin' in de shade and watchin' it all happen."

"I guess I *will* be limin'," Stephen agreed.

"He's going liming at the beach so he can find bimbos in bikinis," Janet said.

The woman threw back her head and laughed, then gave Stephen a conspiratorial wink. "Yeah, mon. You be limin' real good."

"Thanks a lot," Stephen said as they walked away from the cart.

"Just trying to be *sweet*," Janet replied, then ordered, "Take your aspirin."

There were no benches in the area so they took refuge in the shade of an awning outside a shop window while they drank the bottles of juice.

"Does your leg hurt a lot?" Janet asked.

Stephen shrugged. "Aspirin will take care of it."

Sensing her concern, he added reassuringly, "It's only because it's still stiff from the cast. Once I've moved around on it awhile, it'll be as good as new."

But not exactly the same, he thought bitterly. The deep red of the surgical scar would fade with time, but the scar itself would remain to remind him of his own mortality.

"We should have taken a cab," she said a few minutes later. The condition of the sidewalk was deteriorating as they approached the bus area, making walking difficult. High on tourist's adrenaline, she'd scarcely noticed the inconvenience as she'd headed into the shopping district earlier. Now she was acutely aware of the cracks that required constant sidestepping and the rubble that shifted underfoot.

Though he was making a gallant—and slightly macho—effort to hide it, Stephen was suffering with every step. She saw the twitching of muscles in his cheek as he trudged forward, heard him gasp or grunt involuntarily when a loose chunk of concrete gave way under his foot, forcing him to shift his weight abruptly in order to maintain his balance.

Finally she stopped. "I'm sorry. I didn't think . . . look, I could walk back to the taxi stand and get a taxi while you wait here for us to—"

Stephen, who had bent to massage his leg from thigh to knee to calf and back, looked up at her, his face set in grim determination. "We got this far, we might as well go for it." He tilted his head toward the line of buses a block up the street and smiled reassuringly. "We're almost there."

Two buses were pulling out of the lot by the time they reached the boarding area. "What are we looking for?" Stephen said, scanning the destination signs on the fronts of the buses.

"I don't know," Janet said.

"You don't know?"

Sensing a hint of impatience in the question, she looked up at him with a sheepish expression on her face. "All the buses leave from this area, so we just have to ask which one goes to the Rockley."

"Is that all?"

"Well, it can't be too complicated. Any driver should be able to tell us."

He said something that sounded like "Humph." It also sounded quite skeptical.

"For Pete's sake," she said. "I'll go ask. You just stand here and be limin' awhile."

She went to the closest bus and conversed with the driver for what seemed to Stephen to be an awfully long time. Their conversation was animated, with Janet smiling and bobbing her head and then listening with rapt attention as the driver answered her, gesturing with wide sweeps of his arms as he spoke. Janet spoke again, and the driver nodded then pointed down the row of buses. They both laughed just before Janet turned and started walking back toward Stephen. Her laughter faded into a gentle smile as she approached.

"Mission accomplished," she said. "It's the third bus down the line."

"You two had quite a chat," he observed as they headed for the proper bus.

"We had something of a language problem, mon. English may be the native language here, but there's a strong island patois. The only word he understood was Rockley."

She cast a sideway glance at Stephen. His limp was much more pronounced than it had been earlier. "Your leg is really hurting, isn't it?"

"The walk," he said. "I'll be fine when we sit down."

"Then let's get aboard," she said, and then gasped softly as they approached the bus. "I don't believe it! It's the same bus I rode in on, the same driver. Remember, I told you the driver had a stereo system and played calypso rock?"

"Oh, goody!"

"Are you this cranky when you're not in pain?" Janet asked.

Stephen frowned. "No. Actually, I'm not. I'm usually quite a charming fellow. There's a waiting list for the skiing lesson I teach, because I'm so charming."

"I'll just bet," Janet said. *Poor baby. Such a delicate male ego.* She sighed philosophically and wrapped her arm around his, letting the side of her breast press against his bicep as she helped him maneuver the steps onto the bus.

"I'll bet every one of those prospective students is female," she said, and to his affronted look, added, "Not all your charm is hidden inside, Don Juan. You ain't too shabby."

The driver of the bus was rocking in his seat, keeping time to the calypso beat blasting through the stereo sound system. He nodded a greeting as Stephen and Janet boarded, then smiled widely and pointed a finger at Janet. "De Rockley, right?"

"Right," Janet agreed, almost shouting to make herself heard over the music.

"Right," the driver said. "I tell you one stop before."

"Thanks, mon," Janet said.

There were three other passengers already on the bus, each seated next to a window, hoping in vain for some hint of breeze to relieve the stifling heat. Stephen and Janet made their way to the rear of the bus, where the music wasn't so loud. Janet slid into a seat, and Stephen, favoring his leg, landed next to her with a plop.

Tilting his head back, he closed his eyes and heaved a sigh of relief to be off his feet. After a couple of deep breaths, he opened his eyes and settled into a more comfortable position. "This place is an inferno."

Janet checked the window to be sure it was open as far as it would go. "It'll be cooler when we start moving."

"It couldn't get any hotter."

With a growing sense of guilt, Janet observed Stephen's attempt to situate his healthy leg in a comfortable position. "I guess I didn't notice how little legroom there was between the seats," she said lamely.

"A person with short legs wouldn't," Stephen said. His injured limb was still stretched out in the aisle.

Janet thought it politic not to point out that it was not so much that her legs were particularly short as that his legs were unusually long. Instead she asked, "Are the aspirin working?"

"It doesn't hurt now that I'm sitting down. But the itching is driving me crazy. The heat makes it worse."

"Poor baby," she murmured. "This is quite a switch from a Canadian winter, isn't it?"

"They have two inches of fresh powder at home," he said. "I checked the paper this morning."

Digging through the plastic shopping bag that she'd consigned to the floor, Janet drew out the paper bag that held the sachets she'd bought, dumped the sachets into the plastic bag and accordion-folded the empty paper bag into a makeshift fan. She fanned Stephen's flushed face. "Better?"

His hand flew up to catch her wrist. "You don't have to—" He lost his train of thought when his sudden movement positioned his thigh against hers.

"Sorry," she said, wondering when the seat had gotten so narrow, the air so thick and Stephen so imposing.

Stephen's mouth drooped into a frown, and his hand fell away from her wrist. "I already have a mother, and I certainly don't need another sister."

"Sorry," Janet said. "It was a reflex action." Feeling a blush rising in her cheeks, she turned toward the window so he couldn't see her face. She crossed her legs, taking her thigh out of contact with his. Unfortunately, the new position wedged her hip against his hip, and she was more aware than ever of the masculine heat of his body so close to hers.

Outside, a young woman with her hair braided into cornrows and decorated with colorful beads was selling paper cones of crushed ice topped with syrup. Dozens of tiny bees swarmed around the syrup dispensers on her small push cart, but the woman paid them no heed, except when one flew close enough to her face to merit a swat of her hand.

Janet was staring at the bees, marveling at their energy and tenacity, when she became aware of movement beside her. Stephen touched her upper arm to draw her attention. She turned her head slowly to look at his fingers curled around the bare skin just below the armhole of her sleeveless shirt. His skin was rougher than hers, his flesh seemed warmer. Slowly, courageously, she lifted her eyes to meet his, knowing even before she did so that he was already watching her, waiting.

Like his fingers on her arm, his gaze was warm as it locked with hers. His smile was surprisingly gentle. "I'm very glad you're not my sister," he said, then leaned forward and gave her a fleeting kiss.

So am I, she thought, thrilling to the responses of her body to the brief brush of his lips across hers. She'd always wanted a brother, but when a woman found herself in the company of a sexy hunk while on a Caribbean island paradise, she was more in the market for a lover than a sibling. Janet was beginning to feel as though she'd stumbled into her own island fantasy.

The bus's engine ground to life, adding a loud purring accompaniment to the calypso rock still blaring from the stereo system. Lurching and bumping, the bus pulled out of the parking area. Caught off guard, Janet grabbed for the seat in front of her as her hip rubbed against Stephen's with every bounce.

Noting the hard set of his mouth, she asked, "Does the motion bother your leg?"

"No. It's just itching horribly."

"Those starched pants must be like a steam cabinet," Janet said, suppressing the urge to reach over and roll up the leg of his pants to let air around the scar. "You were wise to buy some shorts."

Oh, yes. Very wise. Now everyone on Barbados would be able to view the scarred remains of Stephen Dumont's leg. On the other hand, he thought, frowning, it might be worth putting his scar on public display if it meant an end to this accursed itching.

"We're not going to be doing any eavesdropping," he predicted. Only two other passengers had boarded since he and Janet, and the nearest was four seats in front of them.

"We'll just enjoy the scenery, then," Janet said. A few minutes later, she inhaled sharply as they passed within inches of a beverage truck.

"What was that you said about enjoying the scenery?" Stephen teased.

"I can't get used to riding on the left side of the road," she said. "And the streets are so narrow."

"The cars are smaller than in America," Stephen said. "It's the same in Europe."

The bus pulled over at the first of many stops. Two of the original passengers go off, and several people got on, including three children in gabardine uniforms.

"Oh, look," Janet said. "School must be letting out. Aren't they darling? I read that the Barbadian government established school uniforms so that there would be less class discrimination in the schools between the rich and the poor."

The bus stopped again almost immediately. One person exited and a dozen more uniformed students boarded, chattering and giggling. Two boys dashed up the aisle to claim the rear seat, hurdling over Stephen's injured leg like runners at a track meet. Stephen cringed involuntarily, and almost as involuntarily, Janet found herself wrapping her fingers around his forearm.

"Maybe this was a mistake," she said. "Do you want to get off at the next stop and see if we can call a taxi?"

Stephen cocked an eyebrow at her. "What? Just when we're finally going to have an opportunity to eavesdrop on the natives?"

Another dozen students boarded at the next stop, and the driver raised the volume of the stereo so the music could be heard over the animated chatter of the students, who seemed ready to explode with all the energy they'd kept bottled up during the school day. Three more boys went sailing over Stephen's leg en route to the back seat, which spanned all the way across the rear wall and seemed to be a place of honor reserved for the Bajan version of the hottest dudes in school. Unfortunately, a fourth boy misjudged the altitude necessary to clear the leg and landed a foot squarely on Stephen's tender skin.

Stephen gasped and grabbed his leg protectively. The child who'd stumbled over him froze, eyes widened in terror, while Stephen muttered a string of blistering expletives in two languages which, luckily, were largely drowned out by the music. Finally Stephen noticed the child and gestured him on with a flick of his wrist and a hoarse, "It's okay."

The boy scurried gratefully to the far end of the long back seat, well out of Stephen's line of vision.

"Is it bad?" Janet asked, raising her voice to be heard over the din in the bus.

The scowl Stephen turned on her was intimidating. "Now I'm not so worried about the itching."

"Oh, Stephen," she said. "I'm sorry. We should have—"

"Don't," he said, packing the word with warning as he thrust his face toward hers. His scowl was even more fierce than before, and Janet found herself backing away from him until her shoulder was pressed against the window.

Suddenly realizing how ludicrous the situation had become, Stephen harrumphed disgustedly and let his shoulders fall back against the seat.

The bus stopped.

"Do you want to get off?" Janet asked.

"No," Stephen said. "We must be close to the Rockley by now."

"We could trade places," Janet said. Stephen's brow furrowed as he struggled to hear her. "Trade places," she repeated, louder and gesturing. Dipping her mouth close to his ear, she said, "Your leg will be more protected if you're sitting on the inside."

They switched places while another ten students, these older than the previous ones and wearing uniforms of a different color, filed onto the bus. Most of the seats were filled by the time the bus resumed its route, and some of the students opted to stand rather than sit. They swayed in time to the music.

Three stops later the bus was filled to capacity and beyond. The seats were full, the aisles were packed and the noise level was approaching that of a jet engine running in a tin building. The temperature was rising rapidly, and the entire vehicle was lurching precariously from side to side as the mass of uniformed humanity swayed to and fro to the beat of Caribbean rock.

Every muscle in Janet's body was tense from trying to keep from shoving against Stephen's leg as the crowd pressed into her on the downbeats.

"Eavesdropping is such fun," Stephen shouted into Janet's ear. When she glowered at him, he laughed aloud and stretched his arm across the seat behind her. She relaxed, letting the crown of her head rest against the crook of his elbow, until a timid tap on her shoulder drew her attention to the girl of about twelve who was standing nearest her in the aisle.

"Rockley," the girl said, pointing in the general direction of the door.

"Oh," Janet said, nodding comprehension. "This is our stop," she shouted to Stephen, then hurriedly gathered her belongings, gingerly reaching behind the ankle of Stephen's injured leg, where one of her shopping bags had migrated.

The bus rolled to a stop, and they stood, ready to exit. The driver turned and gave them a thumbs-up and smiled broadly. They read his lips rather than heard him say, "Rockley, mon."

The kids were as accommodating as conditions allowed, turning sideways and scrunching even closer together to open a passageway for Janet and Stephen as they shouldered their way to the door. It was still treacherous going though, and Janet was sure she'd have a few bruises from the short walk.

And if it was bad for her, she thought, it must be miserable for Stephen, whose leg must be getting jostled and pummeled in the crush. She was vastly relieved when they reached the door and she was able to help him down the steps.

They waved goodbye to the driver, the kids and the calypso music, then as the bus disappeared from sight, Janet turned to Stephen. "Are you all right? Your leg?"

"I feel as though I've just parted the Red Sea."

"I'm serious, Stephen."

"How do you suppose they knew who to tell about the Rockley?" he asked.

Janet rolled her eyes in exasperation. Two adult white tourists in a sea of deep brown and indigo-skinned schoolchildren wearing school uniforms? "It was probably our height," she said. "It's a dead giveaway every time."

"Our height, of course," he said. "I should have figured it out."

"Are you able to walk on that leg?"

"If I can't, will you carry me?"

She exhaled a sigh of impatience. "I could walk up to the lobby and have them send a golf cart."

"But that would take so long," he countered. "You could use the fireman's hold—just drape me over your shoulder." He gave her a smug, charming smile. "Think of the possibility for fun if you fell, and we—"

"Either walk or sit down," Janet snapped.

He decided to walk, but a few yards up the driveway he stopped and cocked his head, suddenly alert. "Listen," he said.

"What?"

"No music," he said, then laughed aloud at her wide-eyed seriousness.

Janet scowled at him and resumed walking.

Stephen let a minute go by before saying, "I want to thank you for talking me into taking the bus."

Janet ignored him.

"It was one of those rare opportunities to commune with the natives that makes traveling so appealing," he continued. "A truly memorable experience. The type of experience one writes home about."

When she still didn't reply, he said, "I think I'll write to my sisters about it on the postcards. You remember those charming little postcards we found?"

"I wish you'd stop!" Janet said finally. "I can't tell whether you're serious or sarcastic, and I feel bad enough about pressuring you into . . . and now you're *limping* worse than ever, and I'm—"

"Janet." The curtness of his tone stopped her midsentence, and she looked up into his eyes, mesmerized as he moved toward her. She heard the thunk of his cane hitting the earth, then his hands were on her arms, pulling her next to him. His mouth lowered over hers, and his lips touched hers tentatively, even more briefly than during that elusive kiss on the bus.

The kiss deepened yet remained devastatingly gentle, potent with sweetness. When Stephen lifted his mouth from hers, Janet opened her eyes to find him smiling down at her softly. "It was a truly memorable ride," he said, then dropped another brief kiss onto her mouth before bending to retrieve his cane.

"It was that," Janet murmured. Then more audibly, "Do you need some help?"

"No," he said as he straightened and held the cane up. "See, Mom? Got it all by myself."

"I don't mean to mother you," she said. "It really is a reflex action. Because of my job."

"Are you a nurse?"

She shook her head.

"A kindergarten teacher?"

She shook her head again and explained, "Hostess for Special Tours at Disney World."

"And a Special Tour hostess mothers people?"

"I don't mother them, exactly. I just help them out a little when they need help."

"Help them how?"

"However they need to be helped. Mostly it's a mixture of common sense and simple courtesy. You develop a second sense, learn to anticipate problems and take care of them before they escalate into crises."

"And how does a woman get to be a Special Tour hostess?"

"People are my passion, remember?" She paused. "What about you? Do you do anything at the family lodge besides teach women to ski?"

"A job not without its treacherous moments," he reminded her. "But my degree is in management, and I'm in charge of Dumontique, the in-house fashion boutique, and the pro shop."

"So you're not just a pretty face after all."

He gave her a sharp look. "I wasn't aware that rumor was circulating." Though he said it lightly, the strain of walking was audible in his voice. He was trying to hide it, but he was wincing with every step.

"I'd forgotten the driveway was so long," Janet said, taking Stephen's free hand. "Let's get out of the sun awhile." Leading him into the shade of a massive oak tree, she sat near the trunk and patted the ground next to her. "Sit down. Take a load off."

The muscle that flexed in his jaw was the only one he moved. "You're doing it again, Janet Granville," he said. "Only this time you're not mothering me. You're *babying* me."

Janet frowned at him. "I wish you'd quit being such a twit, Mr. Stephen Dumont! You know that leg is killing you, and it's probably swollen, and you really should get off it for a while, but your male ego won't let you admit it. Who are you trying to impress with this tough-guy, invincible-to-pain act anyway?"

"You!" he roared. He sighed in disgust as he scowled down at her. "And I'm not succeeding very well, am I?"

5

"OH, I'M IMPRESSED, all right," she said. "By your pigheadedness."

Janet knew she'd gone a bit too far when he just stood there, glowering at her. Ah, well, she thought, in for a penny, in for a pound. "You may not have that expression in Canada. It means—"

"I know what it means!" he growled.

"Then why don't you just sit down and take the weight off that leg?"

He glared at her a few seconds longer, then with a grunt of acquiescence, he gingerly lowered himself to the ground beside her and gratefully let his shoulders settle against the trunk of the tree. "You're a hard woman to fight, Janet Granville."

"And I thought you thought I was sweet."

"I used to. But that was when I was young and naïve." He'd drawn up his injured leg and was rubbing his shin.

"Here, let me do that," she said. Moving near the foot of his good leg, she carefully wrapped her fingers around the ankle of his injured leg and guided it, with Stephen's begrudging cooperation, across her lap, then massaged his shin gently through the heavy cotton of his pants.

Stephen closed his eyes and let his head fall back against the tree trunk. *Oh, no!* she thought. *You're not getting off that easy, Mr. Tough Guy Canadian Skier.* "You know, Dumont, your secret was out the first time I saw you."

He opened one eye. "What secret is that?"

"That you're a perfectly normal human being."

Stephen looked as though he might interrupt her, so she hurried to add, "Oh, I thought you were big and strong and virile and all that *macho* stuff, but it never occurred to me that you weren't a human being with the standard human vulnerabilities. I mean, I never once thought, 'Here's a superhuman alien from a distant plant who's impervious to pain or fatigue.'"

He'd opened the other eye and was listening with rapt attention. "So what I can't figure out," she went on, "is why big, strong men hate to let on that under certain circumstances—such as when they've had a badly broken leg—they feel pain, or get tired like any other normal human being. Admit it—you'd have walked five miles with your leg killing you every step before you'd have admitted that you needed to stop for a few minutes."

Stephen appeared disinclined to admit anything in the charged silence that followed. His eyes locked with hers a moment, and then he closed them and tilted his head against the tree trunk again. He drew in a deep breath that sounded rather like a sigh of contentment as she slid her hand under the bottom edge of his pants and massaged his aching, itching flesh with gentle fingers.

Minutes passed. Finally he raised one eyelid sleepily and said, "You thought I was virile, huh?"

"The most virile drunk I'd ever seen."

The eye drooped closed and he exhaled heavily. "You just blew it, Ms. Granville. I was beginning to think maybe you were just a little bit sweet after all."

They rested half an hour before walking the last quarter mile of the driveway. As they approached the Rockley's central courtyard, Stephen asked if Janet wanted a drink from the cabana bar.

"I don't think so," she said, "I'm dying to get into my swimsuit and try out the big, beautiful pool just outside the front door of my bungalow."

"That's a cool idea."

"Uh-huh," she agreed. "I'm going to splash around in that heavenly water until I'm utterly refreshed, then I'm just going to lounge around playing tourist until time to dress for dinner."

A footpath crossed the golf course and led to their bungalows, which were in neighboring courtyards. They were nearing the end of the path when she smiled up at him and said, "You could join me."

His first thought was that if he put on his swim trunks, Janet would see his leg: the pallor, the new hair growing in, the purple-red scar. Everyone at the pool would see it. "I think I'm just going to rest awhile," he said. "Prop up my leg, maybe take a nap."

After a pause, she suggested, "Water would probably be soothing to your leg after all the exertion."

"Maybe another day."

Her smile faltered for an instant, then she shrugged philosophically. "See you around, then."

STEPHEN RECLINED ON THE SOFA in the living room of his bungalow, his foot propped on a pillow. He stared at his bum leg, disbelieving that it was part of his body. The scars that had been itching all day stood out purplish red against the white, dead skin that had been bleached by the cast.

The dark hair that had been shaved away during preparation for surgery was growing back. He still remembered the shock of realizing they'd shaved his leg. That seemingly insignificant side effect of his fall had taken on an inflated importance in those first woozy hours after the anaesthetic wore off—probably because his mind was not yet ready to deal with the more critical aspects of his situation.

The medication, though it couldn't entirely obliterate the pain, had disoriented him and impaired his reason. He'd lain there, drug dazed, half thinking, half hallucinating about Joe Namath wearing panty hose and felt violated and emasculated. Remembering that illogical thought progression embarrassed him even now.

His leg was sore from the day's exertion, especially the kick on the bus and the long walk up the Rockley driveway, but propped up and relieved of weight, it no longer throbbed. The itching too was less of a problem since he'd changed into a pair of the shorts he'd bought in Bridgetown. Air, as Janet had informed him, did seem to be an antidote to the itching.

The hottest part of the day had passed, but it was still warm. The front window and double back doors were open to catch any hint of cross breeze. Beyond the double doors, a trio of tall pines framed a view of the Rockley golf course. Black birds lined the wide limbs of the pines, chattering and squawking.

The pervading scenes and sensations of summer gave Stephen an eerie feeling, as though the theme song to the *Twilight Zone* might swell through the air at any moment. January, and he was hot and the birds were twittering and men were playing golf. And in the next courtyard, Janet Granville was splashing around in a swimming pool, probably attracting the eye of every unattached male guest at the Rockley.

Not that she was strikingly beautiful, he thought. While he had no complaints about her dark lively eyes, full lips and slightly pug nose, she didn't have the type of beauty that stopped conversations when she made an entrance at a cocktail party. She was, he decided, pleasantly pretty.

Briefly he wondered what she would look like first thing in the morning, with her dark hair tousled and no lipstick on those full lips. Briefly. Then he forced that speculation out of his mind. She was no bimbo, this Ms. Granville. She'd made that clear from the beginning. And while he doubted she was a virgin, he also doubted she was in the market for a week-long vacation liaison. No, she was the type who went in for commitment in a big way. Big eyes and an even bigger heart—a heart freely given and easily broken.

His backside had sunk into the less than plump pillows of the sofa and struck an unyielding wood frame. He shifted and managed to send a pain shooting through his leg as he tensed the wrong muscle too quickly. Damn, but it was hot.

A cacophony of squawks drew his attention to the lawn outside, where a rangy white cat was charging several crows who'd ventured down out of the pine trees. The crows won the scuffle easily, flying out of the cat's reach and higher, up to the tree limbs.

Stephen chuckled at the cat's forlorn demeanor as she looked around and discovered all the birds gone. Hearing movement inside the bungalow, the cat decided to investigate, and sauntered through the open doors with all the majesty of a monarch inspecting the barracks of the royal guards. She stopped in the middle of the room to eye Stephen critically and swish her tail disdainfully as if to dismiss him, then proceeded to sniff her way around the room, prodding her nose against the furniture and into corners.

She disappeared from view temporarily, checking out the small kitchenette, Stephen supposed, then returned and fixed him with one of those uppity, down-the-nose stares only cats are capable of.

"Don't complain to me," Stephen said as the cat meowed loudly. "I didn't send you any invitations. If you want a saucer of milk, try begging somewhere else."

The cat sat down and crooked her long tail around her body. She licked the pad of her front paw daintily.

"Oh, no, you don't," Stephen said. "Don't expect me to adopt you. Why don't you go to the pool in the next courtyard? There's a woman there who adopts sad cases." He looked at his cast-bleached leg with its surgeon's artwork and frowned. "Yes. I know. I'm one of her sad cases."

His sigh was heavy and forlorn and followed by a cathartic expletive. "I'm talking to a cat!"

He took another long look at his injured leg, then with guarded movements, eased it off the pillow and pulled himself into a sitting position. If not for his damned pride, he could have been in the pool, swimming with a very attractive woman for the past hour, instead of lying on an uncomfortable sofa in this unnatural January heat holding a one-sided conversation with a scrawny stray cat.

Waving his hands, he shooed the animal toward the back doors. "Scat! Out with you!" The cat moved as far as the patio and assumed the same majestic pose she'd struck in the living room, then turned an accusing glower at Stephen.

"Oh, no, my friend," Stephen said, "don't make me a villain. I didn't invite you here or promise you food. I told you to try your luck at the pool in the next courtyard." Just before bringing the doors together in a decisive click, he winked at the cat and whispered conspiratorially, "I'll meet you there."

The last thing Stephen wanted was to put his leg on public display by wearing shorts or swim trunks. His injury was still too fresh, too private. Too embarrassing to a man who'd been whole and unmarked and now was permanently damaged. He did not want people staring at his injuries with morbid curiosity; he did not want pity.

Damn it to hell—the bottom line was that he didn't want to have to deal with the scar at all. He wanted to wake up and find out that the whole episode was a bad dream, that he hadn't fallen, hadn't been hurt, hadn't had his leg shaven, his broken bone wired together and his naïve self-image of himself as a randy, indestructible young buck—the eternal athlete—shattered.

Some of his confidence had been shattered along with the image. Not confidence in himself, but confidence in life itself. Life, to Stephen Dumont, the pampered son of the Dumont clan, had been sweet. A loving family, affluence, good looks and athletic prowess all had come easily to him, as his natural due. Even women had been easy, from giggling schoolgirls to ski groupies to shop girls at the boutique to the wealthy, sophisticated jetsetters who'd found more than a fashionable vacation address at the Chalet Dumont. But now, in the form of a broken leg, life had dealt him an abhorrent, irreversible blow. What he wanted amounted to naught; he could not change what had happened.

Stephen took one last, morbid look at his leg after changing into his swim trunks, and scowled at the ugliness. He couldn't change facts. It was hot, and he'd only be making himself miserable by hiding inside starched cotton twills.

He was spoiled, perhaps a trace arrogant, but he'd never been accused of stupidity. Or masochism. He'd wear the damned shorts. And as long as he was going to put his new scars on public display, he might as well give Janet Granville a sneak preview.

Feeling as though he had a blinking neon arrow pointing to the scar on his leg, Stephen tossed a towel over his shoulder and left the bungalow, leaving his cane behind. The couple he passed en route to the pool spoke to him the way tourists speak to other tourists in a strange country, but if they noticed his leg, they gave no indication of it. Stephen wasn't sure that counted for much, though, since they obviously were newlyweds and preoccupied in each other's company.

The pool was not crowded. On one side of the shallow end a woman was guiding a toddler through the water, murmuring encouragement at the child's attempts at stroking. A man, probably the woman's husband, lay on a nearby chaise reading a paperback novel.

Janet was sitting on the bank of steps at the opposite side of the shallow end, holding an inflatable beach ball. Though her hair was wet and clung slickly to her scalp, Stephen recognized her instantly and paused to observe her while she was still unaware of his presence. Her swimsuit, while hardly a bikini, was revealing. Her back was bare except for several narrow straps that crisscrossed her shoulders, and the way the bodice exposed the side of her breast made him want to touch her there.

Stephen drew in a breath and put the thought aside. He hadn't come here to seduce here—he'd considered then discarded that idea. He'd come because he was lonely for her company. With a large family and the extended family of guests that kept the Chalet Dumont filled to near capacity year-round, he was not accustomed to being alone.

"How's the water?" he asked upon reaching the pool's edge.

Surprised, she turned and flashed him a brilliant smile, then launched herself from the steps, propping her chin against the ball and hugging it in her arms so that her head stayed above water. "Absolutely wonderful!" she replied sensually.

"Not too cold?" he asked, gingerly maneuvering onto the top step so that the water slapped around his ankles.

"Dis is Barbados, mon. De water never too cold."

Knowing he was putting his leg directly in her line of vision, he took another step. She didn't cringe; in fact, she didn't seem to notice the scar at all.

"Decided to give it a try, huh?" she said. "You won't be sorry."

"I don't think I will," Stephen agreed, perusing her body through the clear pool water. The edge of her suit dipped two inches below her waist, emphasizing the concave curve at the small of her back. When she stretched her legs behind her, he noticed the half-inch moons of pale flesh on her buttocks and upper thigh, and only an iron self-control prevented him from commenting mischievously that her suit must be new.

He sat down on the steps, submerged to the waist. Like a frolicking sea mammal, Janet splashed water high enough to drench his chest. "Come on in, Dumont. The water's perfect."

"What happened to lounging around like a tourist?"

"Boring," she said, in a singsong manner.

"You play Flipper," he said. "I'll just sit here and be boring."

"Not a chance," she said, and tossed him the beach ball. A few strokes brought her back to the steps, and she sat down next to him. "I'm not going to be a martyr. We'll both play tourist."

Tilting her head back, she pointed her face toward the sky. "I love this time of day," she said, sucking in a deep breath. The motion of her chest gave him an incredible view of the cleavage displayed by the deep V of her suit. To divert his attention, he forced his gaze higher, only to find the sight of her neck, so exposed and vulnerable because of the angle of her head, equally provocative.

"How's your leg?" she asked.

Her voice interrupted his speculation on the sensual possibilities of tracing the smooth cords of her wet throat with his tongue. He blinked back to attention. "Hmm? Oh, it's better. I propped it up awhile."

"Let's see the battle scars," Janet said, cupping his ankle with her hand in an effort to guide his leg forward to examine it.

Stephen froze, turning his ski-developed muscles to stone, then winced as pain shot through his calf and streaked up his thigh in reaction to the sudden tautening.

A horrified expression passed across her face. "Did I hurt you?"

"No. I—"

"Are you sensitive about it? The way it looks?" She said it as though she found the concept unbelievable.

Bingo, Ms. Granville.

When he didn't reply, she said. "It's only a scar."

It was his turn to be incredulous. "Only a scar?"

"Didn't you ask the doctor how many stitches it took to sew it up, and whether he used stitches or staples?"

"No."

"Good grief, Dumont, how do you expect to swap war stories if you didn't get the gruesome details?"

"I didn't want the gruesome details. I don't know why anyone would want to know such a thing."

"Stats," she said.

"Stats?"

"Statistics. How do you expect your broken leg to compete with anyone else's if you don't have your statistics?"

"You make it sound like a game. A contest of some sort. My leg was cut open from the knee almost to the ankle. That wasn't any game."

"Of course it wasn't," Janet said, flushing with embarrassment. "But it's healing now, and I thought . . ."

"It's ugly," he said.

"But it's macho," she said. "Surely you've got other scars."

He held up the index finger on his left hand. A thin line ran from his second knuckle to his first knuckle. "My hand slipped once when I was scaling a fish."

Janet grabbed his finger, kissed the minuscule scar and giggled. "Poor baby."

He'd been wrong about Janet. She didn't have a big, generous heart. She was callous and cruel. "Are you having fun, laughing at me?"

"No!" she said. "I'm not laughing at you. Of course I'm not laughing at you. I wouldn't laugh . . . it's just . . . you were so serious about your finger."

"I'm even more serious about my leg. It's grotesque."

"It only seems that way to you, because you're not used to it yet. By this time next year, you won't think any more of it than you do the scar on your finger. As scars go, it's not really all that imposing."

"But it's there!" he said.

"Yes, it's there. But it's only a scar, and it isn't even where people will see it very often. You're healing. You can walk, and in a few weeks you probably won't even limp."

She was staring at the beach ball as though she suddenly found it fascinating. "I'm sorry. It's just that I see people all the time who are so much worse off. It didn't occur to me that a man like you . . . that you'd be sensitive about a scar."

She was still staring at the ball. Stephen studied her face, trying to put the odd conversation into perspective. She looked stricken now, as though she'd accidently kicked a puppy and made it yelp. He raised his hand and pushed a strand of wet hair off her cheek. "What did you mean about seeing people who are worse off?"

"My job," she said softly, without looking up.

"Special guests," he said, comprehending suddenly.

"Last month I took a young man through the park. Just a kid. He was driving home from a high school basketball game when a drunk driver plowed into his car." She raised her eyes to his. "I think he'd be more than happy to have a scar like yours instead of what he has to live with. Even if your leg never got one bit better than it is now, you can walk. You can feel the pain. You—"

She turned her head away from him. After a strained silence, she said in a near whisper, "I'm sorry. That wasn't fair."

Another strained silence followed. Then, staring off into space, he said softly, "Ever since I came out from under the anesthesia, people have been telling me how lucky I was. Lucky that I didn't lose the leg. Lucky it wasn't my spine. Lucky it wasn't my head or my neck. But I didn't feel very lucky. I felt—"

"Hurt," she said, raising her head again. "Because you *were* hurt."

He sighed. "They
it could have been, b
happen at all. I didn't u
to say until now."

He laughed softly, a gent
laughter. "I thought I was inv
was Dumont."

He looked at her and smiled sadl
'of the mountain,' you know. Dum tum-
bling down mountainsides like discarde ans. They
glide down them with the grace of birds flight. It's a
thing of beauty to see. My father was an Olympic medalist. Seventy-five years old, and he's never had a broken bone in his body. I was Canadian downhill
champion, and at thirty-two, I was pushed down the
bunny slope by a giggling fifteen-year-old girl."

"There is no justice in the world," Janet said.

"You're making fun of me again."

"Looking at it as an impartial observer, I'd say that
even considering your broken leg, your balance sheet still
looks pretty healthy overall."

"Balance sheet?"

"Not money. I didn't mean it literally. I was talking
about your overall balance of assets and liabilities.
You've got a lot going for you, you know."

He cocked an eyebrow. "There's always my impressive virility."

"Oh, yes, there's that," she agreed. "That, and your
work at the Chalet Dumont, which you obviously love,
and your sisters, who obviously care about you,
and—"

"And beautiful women who rescue me at airports."

She grinned slyly. "That's a side effect of the virility
factor."

helped me if I'd been homely?" he

d have been more likely to *find* help for you if
d been less . . . respectable looking. You didn't fit the image of skid-row bum, so I gave you the benefit of the doubt and stuck my neck out. I'm lucky you weren't a psychopathic killer."

"How do you know I'm not?" he asked with a grin so winning she'd have doubted him capable of murder even if she'd found him standing over a body with a bloody knife in his hand.

"Should I call the Banff police and inquire about unsolved homicides in the area?"

"For a woman with a big heart, you sure are a brat!"

"Brat?" She grabbed the beach ball, bashed him over the head with it, then tossed it to the opposite end of the pool. "Race you to it," she said, surface diving from the step.

Stephen folded from the waist and lunged under the water, pulling himself along with breaststrokes. Despite her head start and mobility advantage, he reached the ball only seconds behind her and, catching her off guard, managed to volley it back to the shallow end. They chased it from end to end several times and finally collapsed on the steps again, huffing for air and laughing.

"It feels good to move around again," Stephen said.

"How's your leg?" Janet asked.

Stephen's face registered the surprise of a child whose loose tooth has come out painlessly while eating a peanut butter sandwich. "I forgot about it," he said. "I'm sure I've been kicking it some, but it doesn't hurt."

"You aren't putting weight on it when you're swimming."

Stephen laughed aloud. "I'll be damned!"

"Could be why your doctor recommended swimming," Janet said.

"Maybe the old boy wasn't a charlatan after all."

Janet leaned over and kissed his cheek sweetly. "And maybe your sisters weren't so far off-base sending you here, either."

"I'm still going to send the postcards."

Janet laughed at his petulance. "You make them sound like Cinderella's stepsisters, and I'll bet they're perfectly nice, charming women."

"Ha!"

"I'll bet I'd like them if I met them."

"It scares the hell out of me to think how much they'd like you."

"You should bring them to Florida sometime, let me show them Disney World."

"I'd sooner take up skydiving without a parachute. It would be safer."

Ignoring him, Janet reached for his arm and turned the face of his watch toward her. "What time is it? I hope this is waterproof."

"I'm a skier. It has to be waterproof."

"And shock resistant?" she asked drolly. "I didn't realize it was so late. I've got to go. I'm about to turn into a prune anyway."

He gave her a lecherous look. "No way. A mermaid, maybe."

"You'd better hope not. You know what happens to men who look at mermaids the way you're looking at me."

"I'll take my chances."

"You're safe for the time being. I've got to shower and get my hair done before dinner."

"Going anywhere special?"

"Just to the central courtyard for the Bajan buffet."

"Going with anybody special?"

That charming smile again! Janet pretended to consider the question before answering. "I thought maybe I'd run into some other tourists. Maybe socialize a little."

She could smile, too, and be as coquettish as he was charming.

"How would you like to keep a Canadian tourist company?"

"Any particular Canadian?"

"One who'll be lonely if you refuse."

"Lonely, my Great-Aunt Minerva!" Janet said. She climbed the steps and picked up her towel, enjoying the way he watched her appreciatively as she moved.

"Devastated!" he assured her. "Desolate!"

Janet wrapped the towel around her shoulders. "You could scout around for a bimbo or two," she suggested. "I'm sure there'd be fertile pickings for a virile man like you."

"I'd rather waste away of melancholia first," he said.

"I didn't rescue you last night just to have you waste away on me. I'll meet you in the courtyard."

Despite its smugness, his broad smile of triumph pleased Janet, and she was certain she could feel the heat of his gaze on her backside as she strode to her bungalow, swinging her hips just a little more than was frankly necessary.

6

Dear Claire,

Barbados is as hot as hell. Wish you were here sweating and I was in Canada.

STEPHEN CONSIDERED the sentence he'd just written on the postcard and felt slightly dishonest. Twelve hours earlier, it would have been true; he'd have much preferred to change places with Claire. Now . . .

He smiled, then whistled contentedly as he wrote, "No bimbos so far" on the card. That much, at least, was accurate. Janet Granville was no bimbo—and the week he'd been sentenced to spend exiled on the island suddenly held a promise of paradise.

He reached the courtyard early, found a seat and drummed his fingers on the table impatiently as he waited for her. A broad, involuntary smile came over his face when he spied her, prettier than ever in a bright pink cotton shift with a crocheted-lace neckline. In the waning light of the setting sun, she looked sweet and feminine, and by the time he'd watched her cross the courtyard, he could have taken her to bed and not been ashamed of the dimensions of his readiness.

They went to the buffet tables immediately, where waiters in white shirts were serving from chafing dishes piled high with traditional Bajan food.

"What is this?" Janet asked as a waiter placed a square that looked somewhat like a breaded veal cutlet on her plate.

"Flying fish," he said.

"No resemblance to his celebrity cousin on the postcard," Stephen murmured close to Janet's ear.

"Thank goodness," she replied.

They continued down the table, amassing a mountain of food on each of their plates: rice and peas, spiced yams pressed into sausage skins, baked breadfruit with Creole sauce and chicken broiled on open-flame grills. Then came the adventure of testing the flavors and textures of the food. They found the flying fish mild, the yams spicy, the Creole sauce hot and well flavored. Breadfruit turned out to be worthy of its name, since it tasted uncannily like bread, despite its smooth texture.

"Brought to Barbados by the infamous Captain Bligh, captain of the *Bounty*," Janet said as though quoting from a script.

"I beg your pardon?"

"According to the magazine supplied by the hotel, the breadfruit was brought to the island by Captain Bligh. He might have been despised by his crew, but he is beloved by the Barbadians for bringing the breadfruit here." He gave Stephen a wry smile. "You haven't been doing your homework, Mr. Canadian Tourist."

"You're the tourist," he reminded her. "I'm here under duress."

"Oh, yes. I forgot. Torture by tropics."

"I may perish from the persecution."

"Quit whining and finish your flying fish. They're about to start the show."

A portly man, bullish as a prize fighter, mounted the bandstand, welcomed everyone and introduced himself as the manager of the Rockley. Then he introduced Regina, the guest relations manager who'd arranged the tour for Stephen. She was stunningly attired in a floor-length dress of ivory gauze and lace that contrasted dramatically with her ebony skin. Tall, rail thin, she'd added an additional two inches to her impressive height by sweeping her hair atop her head into a mass of curls that cascaded to her shoulders.

She stepped up to the microphone and responded to the oohs and aahs from the crowd with a melodious voice, heavily weighted by the island patois. "Once a week I get to be glamorous, t'anks to our many sponsors. Tonight our fashions are from . . ." She named the boutique, gave its location on the island, then went on to describe the dress she was wearing before signaling for the taped background music and introducing the first model.

"Oh, to be six inches taller and have a six-figure annual income," Janet said later, when a model floated down the runway in a frothy silk-screened evening gown.

"You like that one?" Stephen said.

"I like all of them. There's a distinctly European haute couture flavor to them. I've noticed the European influence all over the island, even among the shop girls." She turned to face Stephen. "You must be more used to that in Canada than we are in Florida."

"People don't dress well in Florida?"

"They dress well, just differently. Florida chic, not Paris chic. The residents wear summer-weight clothing almost year-round. The tourists wear everything, all of it brand-new. And the snowbirds! Polyester pantsuits, short—and I do mean *short*—shorts and high heels."

"I like the way you dress," Stephen said, testing an opening in the lace on her shoulder to see if it was wide enough to allow his forefinger contact with her skin. He moved closer to her than was strictly necessary and whispered sensuously into her ear. "I like the way you smell."

Janet inhaled sharply as his breath fanned over her neck, "It's the finishing lotion I put on my hair."

"I like your hair, too." Looking directly into her eyes, he slowly lifted a curl from her cheek and rolled it between his thumb and fingertips as though savoring every nuance of texture. His smile was warm enough to melt a polar ice cap.

Janet would have loved to come up with some clever little snippet of repartee, but she discovered she was speechless in the heat of such deliberate seduction. She had fantasized about meeting a gorgeous male and having a passionate holiday affair, but she'd never in her wildest imaginings believed she would actually be looking into the eyes of a flesh-and-blood man like Stephen Dumont on the evening of her first full day on Barbados. The odds against meeting such a man on vacation were astronomical; she'd been smugly secure in the impossibility of her fantasy coming true when she'd joke so blithely with Trudy about a vacation love affair.

While the fantasy was universal, the reality of Janet Granville's life was that she was not a likely candidate to go to a Caribbean island and have a holiday fling with a relative stranger. She had made many good friends through her job and led an active social life that included jaunts to the entertainment attractions abounding in Florida, as well as the standard gamut of movies and concerts and festivals. But her last lover had been the almost-financé she'd left behind in Minnesota.

There had been no one special—special enough—in her life since she'd moved south. She shared a double-wide with her mother in a mobile home park populated mostly by retirees, and so far she hadn't noticed that living with her mother was crimping her love life any. When she'd joked about a vacation lover, she'd truly been joking.

But now, with Stephen Dumont peering into her eyes and turning on the heat with the sexiest smile since Errol Flynn's swashbuckling heydays, the idea didn't seem so much like a joke.

A burst of applause signaled the end of the fashion show and brought Janet and Stephen back to an awareness of their surroundings. Stephen, still smiling, dropped the lock of hair he'd been holding and sat back in his chair. Janet turned her attention to the runway, where the models were lined up in all their finery, and joined in the applause.

The runway was dismantled quickly, and a small band complete with steel drums set up on the bandstand. After the group's introductory song that combined calypso, reggae and rock, the bandleader, who was dressed in white pants that reached just below his knees and a brilliant red cummerbund, recruited two cane holders from the audience.

To a primitive beat from the steel drums, he bent backward to demonstrate the limbo, slithering under the poles, first when they were about waist high, then again and again, having the cane holders lower the pole each time until they had to kneel for comfort as they held the cane mere inches above the ground.

It seemed to the audience that surely no human being would be physically able to bend low enough to pass beneath it. But the musician, his body honed over years of practice to achieve superhuman contortions, shimmied beneath the pole, propelling his nearly prostrate form along with tiny hops that progressed him inches at a time. The second his head had cleared the pole, he lunged upright, then bowed, accepting the audience's applause with a wide sweep of his arm and a triumphant smile.

He took a microphone held out by one of the other band members and said, "Now dat you've seen how simple it is, we have a limbo contest."

There was no rush of contestants, so Regina circulated among the tables to recruit some. She paused at Stephen and Janet's table and lifted an eyebrow at Stephen. Laughing, he picked up his cane and pointed to his leg while shaking his head. Regina's querying gaze turned to Janet then, who lifted the bottom edge of her dress daintily and shook her head, as well.

"I think you should have gone," Stephen said after Regina had moved on to another table.

"In a dress?" Janet replied.

"We could have set up a camera, made a companion postcard for the one I sent to Brigitte. Man doing limbo. Woman doing limbo."

Janet glared at him menacingly for a few seconds, but his charm was irresistible, and she was unable to hold on to her pique in the face of it. Finally she sighed in defeat. "I'll bet your mother has tales to tell about raising you."

"I was a model child," he said, as though offended by the implication he could have been otherwise.

Janet's humph was succinct. Stephen laughed, put his arm across her shoulders and gave her a hug. He left his arm draped over the back of her chair while they watched the limbo contest. Several contestants had been recruited, and the band resumed playing while they lined up and easily walked under the cane that was being held at shoulder level.

After four or five passes, when the cane hovered about a yard above the ground, one contestant was eliminated. The same thing happened at the next two levels until a banker from New Jersey was declared champion and awarded a bottle of the island-made rum for his achievement.

Cheering the contestants on and laughing at their less than successful attempts to pass under the cane poles at the lower levels had loosened up the crowd. When the band resumed playing island music, many of the guests ventured to the dance floor to work off the heavy Bajan buffet with whatever step seemed appropriate.

Stephen and Janet sipped rum punch, listened to the music and watched the dancers, since the volume of the music precluded conversation. After a dozen songs, the bandleader announced that they would play a special request. Scattered applause broke out when the audience identified the Caribbean perennial "Yellow Bird."

"At last, something slow," Stephen said. He leaned to whisper into Janet's ear, "I probably won't be very graceful, but if you'd like to give it a try. . ."

They stood. Stephen was holding his cane in his right hand. Looking up into his eyes, Janet put her hand over his and gently opened his fingers so that she could take the cane away and prop it against his chair. "You won't need this," she said, guiding his arm across her shoulders so she could brace him if necessary.

The music was not ideal, and Stephen's leg restricted his movement, but Janet and Stephen neither noticed nor cared. His arms were around her shoulders, Janet's around his waist.

"I've been wanting to feel you in my arms all evening," he murmured. Janet hugged his waist a little tighter and snuggled her cheek against his chest contentedly. He responded by pressing his cheek into her hair.

Again Janet experienced the odd sensation that she'd danced into her own island fantasy. In a movie the music would be turning orchestral and swelling with intensity while stage fog enveloped them. That was the feeling: ethereal, dreamlike, ecstatic. The textures, scent and warmth of him were muddling her senses into a general awareness of the pleasure of being a woman in a man's embrace.

All too soon "Yellow Bird" ended, and they were jarred back to reality by calypso rock. Lifting their heads, they looked at each other, and Stephen raised an eyebrow skeptically, asking in the simple gesture if she wanted to keep dancing. She shook her head and turned so that his arm was across her shoulders again as they walked back to their table.

A few minutes later, they left the central courtyard. As they crossed the golf course, the whistlelike chirps of the Bajan crickets gradually replaced calypso rock. The sky was clear, the sliver of moon bright white against the indigo sky. They didn't talk, but the pristine touching of their bodies as they walked was enough; the quiet between them was intimate and comfortable.

By night, the courtyard in front of Janet's bungalow was a tropical garden. The water in the pool glistened amid trees and shrubs silhouetted by spotlights tucked under their branches. They passed it by and found privacy in the shadows of the unlighted shrubs that flanked the door to her bungalow.

Stephen propped his cane against the door and raised his free hand to caress her cheek. In the near darkness, Janet could almost believe that nothing existed beyond the shadowed doorstep and the man who was looking down at her face and finding beauty there.

Sliding his fingers into her hair, he tilted her head back and kissed her unhurriedly, as though making a statement that kissing her was of such monumental importance that he refused to be hurried. When he drew away from her, he softened the shock of their parting with another fleeting touch of his lips to hers. Then he wrapped his arms around her and hugged her tightly.

"You hair still smells good," he said after several timeless minutes.

"I'm glad I used the finishing spray."

"I'm glad my sisters sent me to Barbados."

"So am I."

More timeless seconds grew into minutes. Gradually he loosened his embrace. "I hate letting you go. It feels so right having you next to me."

Then don't let me go! Janet thought desperately. *It feels right to me, too.*

But there was a rightness about his letting go of her, too, about the bittersweetness of having to say goodnight. Instead of inviting him inside her bungalow, she said, so low it was barely more than a whisper, "Thank you."

"For what?"

"For...everything," she said, almost sighing the words. "For making my first full day and night on the island...special." Her soft chuckle surprised them both. "I'm sorry about the bus."

"I'm not," he said and then in a caressing tone he spoke her name, "Janet..."

The beautiful way he said it, with that soft trace of a French-Canadian accent, brought her perilously close to wanting to cry. She raised her face and poised her mouth to speak, but found she didn't know what to say. It didn't matter, because he lowered his mouth to hers again and swallowed the unformed words with the ardor of a long-hungry man who'd just found sustenance.

This time when he raised his lips from hers, he placed his hands on her shoulders and subtly drew his body away from hers. "Do you have your key?" he asked with finality.

Nodding, she searched in her purse for it and let him wrestle with the lock. The door opened suddenly, and his cane fell crashing onto the floor of the bungalow. They both scrambled to pick it up, then laughed as their hands closed around it at the same time.

They straightened and sobered. Janet became aware that another opportunity had presented itself for her to invite him in, but when he dangled the key near her hand, she took it without comment. After a strained pause, Stephen leaned forward and kissed her on the forehead. "Good night, Janet."

He waited until she was safely inside and the lock had clicked into place before stepping onto the path that would lead him to his own bungalow.

7

THE NEXT MORNING Janet carried a simple breakfast of juice, cheese and buttered bread out to the small table on the patio behind her bungalow. To her delight, she immediately drew a curious audience of blackbirds, doves and sparrows, all of which eyed *her* warily, and her bread covetously. She finished her own meal, then shredded the heel of the loaf of bread and tossed the crumbs to her feathered guests.

It became quickly apparent that the doves would eat only what she threw directly to them, while the sparrows made rapid diving forays to the tabletop or patio stones to retrieve a promising crumb. The blackbirds, eternal scavengers, stole what the doves missed and gloried in flying off with the larger hunks of crust the smaller birds could only peck at.

Janet was watching a sparrow move tentatively toward a crumb near the edge of the table, when a yellow bird swooped down, seemingly from nowhere, and began munching on it merrily.

"Where did you come from?" she asked, amused by the tiny bird's bravado. The yellow bird simply glared at her brazenly while it finished off the crumb and began looking around for more.

Janet broke up the remaining bread and tossed it out, apportioning it to the different groups and sliding the last few crumbs toward the yellow bird. The yellow bird gave her a stare that seemed to accuse her of stinginess, but

Janet refused to be intimidated. "That's it for this bungalow, kiddo. If you want a five-course meal, fly on over to the central courtyard and raid the syrup pitchers."

She sighed contentedly and thought of the morning before and the yellow bird that had flown onto the table while she and Stephen were talking. "Bold as brass," Stephen had said.

Suddenly solemn, she wondered where Stephen was and what he had planned for the day. Whatever it was, apparently it didn't include her, because he hadn't inquired about *her* plans. It had come as a shock to her when she realized that, after the idyllic time they'd spent together, after the sweet intimacy of their good-night kisses, he hadn't asked to see her again.

But while she went on wildly hoping it had been an oversight and not a deliberate decision not to see her again, she refused to sit around pining after him. She'd come to a paradise island to have fun, and today she was going to the beach, with or without Stephen Dumont.

Unless she ran into him on the way to the lobby and he made a better suggestion.

With the issue of Stephen Dumont firmly resolved, she pulled a pair of shorts and a terry cover-up over her swimsuit, packed her beach bag and headed for the lobby to wait for the next shuttle—hoping all the way that she'd run into Stephen on the golf course or in the central courtyard. She'd run into him by chance in the courtyard yesterday; if he were a creature of habit—and what man wasn't?—he might be there today, as well.

She looked through the long window in the Rockley lobby and surveyed the diners in the central courtyard. But he wasn't there. Then the beach shuttle arrived, and she was forced to abandon her watch at the window and board the van with a honeymooning bride and groom and a slightly older couple herding three rambunctious children.

The contrast between the attitudes and priorities of the honeymooners, oblivious to anyone and anything outside themselves, and the parents, harriedly monitoring their children, was pronounced. *Before* and *after*, Janet thought wryly. But it was difficult to remain detached and acerbic when, in the company of an amorous pair of newlyweds and a classic family unit of mom, pop and kids, she was suddenly acutely conscious of her own solitary state.

Between admonitions to her three children to sit down, keep their hands to themselves and quit arguing, the mother asked Janet, "Is this your first trip to the Caribbean?"

"Yes," Janet said.

"Ours, too. Davey won a sales contest. We were going to leave the kids with my mom—you know, make a second honeymoon of it, but my mom fell last week and broke her leg, and we didn't have anyone else to watch them."

"There seems to be an epidemic of broken legs lately," Janet said.

"She slipped on a patch of ice when she was taking out the trash," the woman volunteered, before giving her eldest child a sharp look. "James Michael, if you can't keep that gum inside your mouth, then I'll give you a tissue to spit it into."

"You must live in the north," Janet said.

"Just south of Chicago," the woman said. "Jamie, quit pestering your brothers."

She shifted her attention back to Janet. "My husband sells commercial trash service—you know, those dumpsters businesses rent. He was the top salesman in the region."

"No one wants to hear about trash, Cheryl," her husband said.

"Oh, but—" Janet began. She was spared having to assure him that she found trash *fascinating* when he turned to his son in exasperation. "Jamie, didn't your mother just tell you to stop that?"

"Some second honeymoon," Cheryl said under her breath as the van pulled into a circular driveway in front of a beachfront lounge. She began collecting the overstuffed tote bags the family had brought. "Everybody got their pail and shovel?" The children nodded in unison and held up plastic beach buckets complete with sand molds and kid-sized shovels.

"Maybe we'll see you again," Cheryl told Janet over her shoulder as she steered the youngest through the van door. "Hold my hand, Kevin, there's a busy road there."

Janet remained seated until the newlyweds had left the van, then climbed out and looked around to get her bearings. The lounge featured a bar and shaded terrace that overlooked the water. Beyond the terrace stretched the Caribbean Sea, as turquoise as the travel brochures had promised. A brilliant sun, azure skies, sailboats on the horizon and a ribbon of white sand punctuated by tall palm trees enhanced the postcard perfection of the view. A dent in the coastline formed a natural basin for swimming, and tourists of all ages and sizes, in all degrees of dress, were splashing and swimming and floating in the water.

Between the narrow bustling street and the sandy shore, a handful of vendors had set up shop. Shirts and drawstring beach pants made from sugar sacks hung from lines stretched between trees in a small copse near the sand, and a short, stout Barbadian woman stood by, ready to answer questions or receive payment for her merchandise. A middle-aged man neatly, if not fancily, dressed in cotton pants and shirt and leather sandals with tire soles tended a stack of folding lounge chairs available for rent. Nearer the street, pushcart merchants offered coconuts, pineapples and bottled drinks.

Janet rented a chaise lounge, found a stingy strip of shade cast by a palm tree, took off her shorts and cover-up and stretched out to read the paperback novel she'd been reserving for her vacation. Half an hour later, toasty warm from the sun, she dashed to the water for a quick swim.

The water was cool, and as soft as satin on her skin. And clear—so perfectly clear. She stood in water up to her shoulders and wiggled her toes and could see her polished toenails fluttering as easily as she would have if looking through a pane of glass.

The shadow of the palm tree had shifted by the time she returned to her chair, so she repositioned the chaise before applying a fresh coating of sunscreen and picking up her book again. She was well into a new chapter when the sound of a throat being cleared purposely usurped her attention.

A woman about Janet's age, petite and shoe-button cute, was standing near the chair. She smiled cheerfully and, sensing that she had piqued Janet's interest, knelt next to the chair. "You want braids?" she asked, patting her own cornrowed hair and smiling. "Caribbean chic."

"I don't . . ."

"I show you," she said. Capturing a narrow strand of Janet's chair, she began French-braiding it. Reaching the end, she held on to it with one hand and dug into a canvas tote bag with the other until she produced a small square of foil. She wrapped the ends of the braid in the foil and then pinched it into a point, which she threaded through a colored bead. The she rolled the end of the foil into a knob that held the bead in place.

"I can make your hair pretty, pretty, pre-tt-y," she said eagerly. "Island style. You keep it dat way on de island."

"My hair's wet," Janet said. "It's full of salt water. I'd have to wash it."

"You wash dem braids, no problem," the woman said.

Her enthusiasm was contagious. Janet had seen a number of tourists with beaded braids, and she'd overheard an expensively dressed woman discussing the fifty dollars she'd spent having her teenage daughter's hair braided at one of the island salons. With that in mind, she asked, "How much do you charge?"

They settled on a price, and the woman, whose name was Alice, "like de Princess Alice highway," quickly went to work. When she'd finished, she dug a hand mirror from her canvas bag and shoved it into Janet's hand. "You like? Dey look pretty."

Janet gave a swish of her head, sending the colorful beads into a chorus of clicks as they tickled over the top of her shoulders. "I look just like Bo Derek," she said, "except that she's taller and thinner and blond. . . ."

Alice laughed. "You like, eh?"

"I like it," Janet agreed. "I look like a bona fide tourist."

"Real Caribbean."

Real Hollywood is more like it, Janet thought. She paid Alice and went back to reading her book, feeling quite touristy.

Deeply involved in the story, she did not realize she'd lost the shade of the palm tree until a shadow suddenly settled across her face and shoulders. "Improving your mind, Ms. Granville?" asked a familiar voice.

"I do read, on occasion," she said, shading her eyes with her hand as she looked up at Stephen's face.

He was staring at her hair. She flicked the braids with a flip of her wrist, setting of a cacophony of clicking. "I've gone native," she said. "What do you think? On a scale of one to ten?"

Awkwardly protecting his injured leg, Stephen carefully lowered himself into the scrub grass next to the chair. Once settled, he reached up and cupped her chin, then tilted her head at various angles.

"Well?" she prompted, prepared for him to say he hated it, because she knew perfectly well that men like a woman's hair long, loose and unencumbered.

He continued staring at her hair, considering it from various angles, then his eyes settled on her face. Settled *warmly* on her face in a way that unnerved Janet and suddenly made the tropical sun hotter, her throat drier, the air thinner.

His voice was husky, with a bedroom inflection. "I think I'd like to be the one to undo it," he said. "Braid by braid."

To *that*, Janet was speechless.

A long moment passed in silence before Stephen said, "I looked for you at the hotel."

"I left early." Had he asked about her at the Rockley desk, been told she'd taken the beach shuttle?

"I overslept," he said, and added with a note of petulance, "I never oversleep."

"Jet lag."

"I don't suffer jet lag when I go to Europe."

"Must be the tropical climate then."

"It *is* hot," Stephen complained. Unexpectedly he grabbed the bottom edge of his shirt and peeled it off over his head.

Janet wolf-whistled softly. "Trolling for bimbos?"

Stephen's only reply was an irritated frown.

"You really should wear sunscreen if you're going to sit outside this time of day. Your face is already showing the sun."

He frowned. "I wear sunscreen all the time on the slopes because of the glare. But—"

"You forgot it at home. No problem, mon," Janet said. "I just happen to have some along."

"Why am I not surprised?" Stephen said while she dug into her beach bag. "I wouldn't be surprised if you pulled a white rabbit out of that bag."

"I'm not into magic," Janet said drolly. "Just sunscreen and meat tenderizer and—"

"Meat tenderizer?"

"You always take meat tenderizer to the beach," Janet said. "In case—"

"In case a tough old codfish leaps at your feet and begs you to fry him?"

"In case of jellyfish," she said sternly. "It neutralizes their sting."

"What's a jellyfish?"

Janet started to explain, and the description of balloonlike fish with long, stinging tentacles sounded preposterous even to her. Then she noticed he was grinning and realized he'd known all along what a jellyfish was. Giving him a piqued frown, she offered him the bottle of lotion.

"Oh, no, Miss Do-gooder," he said as the grin turned leering. "It's your lotion, you rub it in."

"All right," Janet said, "but I'm not waiting for it to warm up in my hand before I put it on."

It turned out to be a moot threat, since the lotion was pleasantly warm from having been in the tote bag in the sun. Stephen fairly purred as she spread it over his back and shoulders, then paid careful attention to the tender skin where his arm joined his shoulder, because that area, easily missed, was particularly prone to sunburn.

She slid her hands straight down under his arms, along his ribs, until she reached the waistband of his trunks and left her hands there, spread motionless over his ribs, and said diabolically, "Maybe I should see if you're ticklish."

"You're welcome to run your hands over my body to test me, but I'm not ticklish," he said.

Drawing her hands back into her own lap, she said, "Other side."

Stephen leaned back against the chair so she could reach his chest. Janet massaged the lotion into the swell of his chest muscles, then leaned forward to reach the area between his ribs and above his navel. Her breasts pressed into his nape, and as he tilted his head back so he could see her face, his hair brushed provocatively against the V above her swimsuit. He smiled up at her smugly.

Janet pulled away from him and dropped the bottle of lotion into his lap. "You can do your own legs."

"Have you been in the water yet?" he asked after finishing with the lotion.

She nodded. "It was glorious. Barbados isn't volcanic, you know. It has a foundation of coral that acts like a giant underwater filtering system."

Stephen harrumphed skeptically. A few minutes later he complained, "It's ungodly hot."

"It's sunny and warm," Janet said, just to be perverse.

"It's as hot as hell," Stephen repeated firmly.

"There's a whole sea out there to cool off in," Janet pointed out.

Stephen frowned at that suggestion.

"Don't you like the beach?" she asked curiously.

"I don't like sand," he grumbled.

"Sand?" she asked incredulously.

"It's disgusting," he said. "It sticks to your feet when they're wet and shifts under your feet in the water and gets . . . *everywhere* inside your clothes and scratches."

Janet rolled her eyes at what she obviously considered frivolous objections.

"If you can hate snow, I can have a strong dislike for sand!" Stephen snapped.

"Oh, go on in. Endure it. Go for a swim. You might stumble over some bimbos in the water."

Stony silence.

"You're already two behind schedule," Janet reminded him.

More stony silence.

"I could go with you," she said. "To help you screen them."

"Screen them for what?"

"Quality, of course," she replied. "Even though you're in a hurry, you mustn't lower your standards. There's nothing more pathetic than a mediocre bimbo."

"You're not going to rest until you get me into the water, are you?"

She feigned outrage. "I was just trying to be helpful. I'm *sweet*, remember? 'As a sugar cookie,' I believe the phrase was."

"Memory like an elephant," he grumbled.

"Where do sugar cookies fit into the big picture?" she asked. "Are they above or below bimbos?"

He ignored the question. After a brief silent, he said, "I'm hungry."

"They're selling coconuts out by the street," she said.

"I don't like coconuts."

"You'd better hope you're never stranded on a desert island," she said, giggling softly. "Oh, you really would be miserable, wouldn't you? All that sand, and all those coconuts, and not a bimbo on the beach!"

"Let's go back to the Rockley for lunch."

"All right," she said. "But not until you at least put a toe in the water."

8

"MY SOCKS ARE FULL of sand," Stephen said.

"We'll be at the hotel in another five minutes," Janet said. "You can change them."

"My shoes will be full of sand. I'll never get all the sand out of my shoes after this. I'm already limping because of my leg, and now my feet will be raw."

Janet drew an imaginary circle on the top of his hand with the tip of her forefinger and smiled coquettishly, trying to woo him out of his snit. "Admit it—wasn't the swim worth a little minor discomfort?"

"This discomfort is not minor," he said, shifting uncomfortably. "I have sand inside my swim trunks."

Janet sniffed in disdain. "Are you this much of a baby when you get snow inside your ski suit and get all damp and cold?"

"They do not make sandpaper from snow," Stephen said. "They make sandpaper from sand, and if you were inside my swim trunks now you would understand why."

"I wish I *were* inside your swim trunks, so you wouldn't have to worry about the damned sand!"

"I'm ready to give it a try," Stephen said. "My bungalow, or yours?"

A blush burned its way up Janet's neck to color her cheeks, and her eyes widened in horrified embarrassment. "I didn't mean that the way it sounded."

Ah, the resiliency of men! In a sudden frenzy of amusement, Stephen appeared to have succeeded entirely in forgetting the sand in his pants. "Oh? And just how do you think it sounded, Ms. Granville?"

"Like something a bimbo would say!"

Stephen laughed. "And to think I just wrote my sisters that I hadn't met a single bimbo on Barbados!"

Janet looked down at the front of her swimsuit. "Sorry, no bikini."

"We could shop for one," Stephen suggested. "A bus to Bridgetown stops at the gate every half hour."

"I've got a better idea," Janet said, picking up her beach bag as the van navigated the circular parking area in front of the Rockley lobby. "Come with me, and I'll show you how to get the sand out of your pants."

"No man could pass up an offer like that," he said. But later, when they'd reached Janet's courtyard and she'd presented him with her magical solution, he was disappointed and skeptical. "The pool?"

"Absolutely," Janet said, putting her thumbs into the elasticized waistband of her shorts. "A quick dip is the best way to get rid of sand and that sticky, salt feeling."

He was standing there, silently watching her.

"Now what's wrong?" she asked.

"Watching you undress is complicating my problem."

"Maybe the water will be cold," she said, smiling sweetly. She tossed her shorts onto the nearest chair and jumped into the deep end of the pool.

"One can only hope," Stephen muttered under his breath, and dropped into a chair to untie his sand-besieged sneakers so he could join her.

AFTER THEIR BRIEF SWIM in the pool, Janet and Stephen had changed into fresh clothes and gone to the Rockley courtyard for a late lunch of fruit and cheese ordered from the cabana bar. Lunch had evolved into lazy hours of people-watching. Then Stephen had invited her to accompany him to a musical review at the Barbados Museum. They had laughed when she told him she already had made reservations for the show through Regina at the guest-relations desk, just as he had.

Most of Janet's prevacation shopping had been for shorts and shirts, but she had found one sundress she couldn't resist, and she decided it would be perfect for their outdoor musical. Classic blue chambray, it was trimmed with a wide band of cotton lace on the skirt and narrow cotton lace on the top edge of the bodice. Three sets of spaghetti straps tied on each shoulder to produce a frilly bow.

She hadn't been sure how to wash her hair while it was braided, so she'd finally poured a large glass of diluted shampoo over the braids, rinsed longer than usual under the shower, then blotted them with a towel. Now that they were thoroughly dry, she sprayed them liberally with the scented finishing lotion that Stephen liked so well.

He commented on the scent while they rode in the chartered bus to the Barbados Museum. The trip itself was not a long one, but the bus made a number of stops that stretched the ride into half an hour. Pressed against Stephen from shoulder to knee in the narrow seat, Janet scarcely noticed the delay.

The first time she'd seen Stephen, she had admired the stark male beauty of him the way one admires art. Now her admiration of him was far from dispassionate. She appreciated not only the form and arrangement of his features, but also the animation of his eyes, the timber of his voice when he spoke, the strength and energy in his lean, fit body.

The virility she had acknowledged in that first appraisal held a different significance for her now; as she had gotten to know him, it had become power instead of just fact. His smile reached the core of her femininity, and she responded to his maleness the way a woman was created to respond to a man, with warmth and a more acute awareness of herself as a woman.

The disorientation of strange surroundings and the change of routine on the island had distorted time. It seemed impossible that only two nights before, the man next to her had been merely a well-dressed, intoxicated stranger, a fellow traveler in need of help. Now he was Stephen Dumont, and she knew about him, his family, his life, his charm, his foibles.

In just two days she had glimpsed the contrasts in him that made him unique: he loved snow but hated sand in his pants; he loved cheese but despised mangoes; he spoke of his sisters as though they were harridans, in a voice rich with affection; he was bright and witty and competent, yet at times he was also, in an endearing, charming way, as petulant as a spoiled little boy.

She'd discovered, too, the many layers of him. While she would categorize him as spoiled rotten because of the affluence into which he was born and the attributes nature had endowed upon him, he was generous and attentive to her needs. He'd shown her in a dozen ways that he found her desirable, but he'd managed to assure her that he enjoyed her companionship as a fellow human being. They were friends—and he would be a thoughtful, caring lover if their relationship progressed in that direction.

Deep in reflection, she didn't hear him speaking to her until he said her name questioningly. Startled to be interrupted while pondering his potential as a lover, she gasped and hoped he wouldn't notice the color rushing to her cheeks. "Did you say something?" she asked.

"I asked if the foliage is thick like this in Florida, even in the winter?"

"Yes," she said, surprised that her voice wasn't shaky. "We have a lot of the same plants, in fact. Palms and hibiscus and crotons and periwinkles and, of course, the ferns and philodendrons. But we don't have the continuous growing season they have here. We do have a winter of sorts, and we usually have one or two mild freezes, so the tropical stuff gets nipped, or goes through a dormant period. Here everything just keeps growing bigger and thicker."

"It still seems peculiar to me, all this greenness in January," Stephen said. "It's as though nature made a mistake. Doesn't it get monotonous when nothing ever changes?"

"I do miss the seasons sometimes," Janet admitted. "The color of the leaves in autumn and the sense of renewal in the spring."

"That's the first thing you've ever said about missing your home."

"No place is perfect. A person has to decide what's most important. I can sacrifice red leaves in October for warm sunshine in November—and December. And January. And February. And March. And—"

"You've made your point," Stephen said.

The bus was slowing and soon parked, and they were led through the double wood doors of a two-story nineteenth-century building that had once housed the military prison of the British garrison. Once inside the museum, they were welcomed and directed to the exhibit area.Stephen reached for Janet's hand in a gesture that was both affectionate and possessive. The pressure of his fingers curled round hers was both reassuring and stimulating. She had felt the masculine roughness of his fingers on her face, her neck, even her back as they had cavorted in the turquoise sea, and now the feel of his hand circling hers set her speculating on what it would feel like to have those fingers touch her in other, tenderer places. The thought made it difficult to concentrate on the artifacts of Barbadian history that filled the museum's exhibits.

Early maps, some dating to the seventeenth century, were displayed in glass cabinets, but it was the people-oriented items that Stephen and Janet found most intriguing. Cotton garments, centuries old, made Janet pause to admire the fineness of the cloth and the hand-worked lace that trimmed it.

"Island-grown cotton, prized throughout the world," Stephen said, summarizing the caption. "Bet it cost a pretty penny back then."

"Drop into any fine lingerie department," Janet said. "Cotton with detail work like this *still* costs a pretty penny."

They moved on to several displays that dealt with the institution of slavery, which had left such marked influences on the history, culture and character of the island. Established on Barbados during the seventeenth century with the importation of slaves from West Africa to work in the sugarcane fields, it was abolished there in

1834—three decades before the American Civil War put an end to slavery in America.

An entire case was devoted to the legend of the tamarind seed, said to resemble a man's head because an innocent man was hung from the limb of the tree that bears it.

"This must be the museum in the movie!" Janet said.

"What movie?" Stephen asked.

"'The Tamarind Seed,'" Janet said. "It was a spy movie, with Julie Andrews and Omar Shariff. They visited the museum and saw the seed and laughed at the legend. Then at the end of the story, when she thought he was dead, he sent her a tamarind seed to let her know he wasn't. It was so romantic."

"They were madly in love, of course," Stephen said dryly.

"It happens to people occasionally, especially in the movies."

"Perhaps it happens to people in this museum," he said, smiling, and the words themselves exuded warmth.

There were a number of maritime exhibits, including a case of "sailors' valentines," wooden boxes intricately decorated with tiny shells that sailors took home to their lovers.

"There's another romantic notion for you," Stephen said.

"The sailors probably kept entire trunks full of them so they could pass them out at every port, like American GIs passing out candy bars in Europe after World War II," she replied.

"What's this? A skeptic?"

"Men will be men," Janet said drolly. "And you know what they say about sailors."

"I'm disappointed in you, Janet. Think about a lonely young man, at sea for months and months with nothing to think of but the girl back home. Imagine him trying to find just the right box for her, one pretty enough for her, with hearts in it to show how much he loved her."

"You're a closet romantic," Janet said. The idea enchanted her.

He squeezed her hand gently and smiled down at her. "Perhaps I'm just particularly aware right now of how a pretty girl can make a man feel."

You're not only romantic, you're sweet, Janet thought as they left the museum. On the patio of the main structure, a dozen or so rows of long tables had been set with white paper tablecloths in preparation for the buffet. Immediately below the patio was a small stage, and beyond that was a courtyard filled with ancient oaks surrounded by tropical shrubs.

In the very center of the yard, black women in traditional cotton dresses, aprons and colorful bandannalike scarves presided over a huge bowl of fruit punch and sweating pitchers of island rum punch.

Flanking the courtyard were two long buildings, also former prison cells. Older than the main structure, which was finished in 1853, they were constructed between 1817 and 1821. These older cells now housed life-size panoramas of typical early plantation life, with furnishings and props representative of the plantation era.

One of the scenes depicted a dining room, the long wooden table spread with a linen cloth and set for a formal meal. "It's so timeless," Janet said. "A family could sit down and eat a holiday dinner there tomorrow."

"Table appointments haven't changed much since the invention of china and flatware," Stephen said.

"But think about it—bone china and silver candlesticks on an island in the middle of the Caribbean Sea, a hundred years before the airplane was invented. All the comforts of civilization."

"Except antibiotics, indoor plumbing and electricity," Stephen pointed out.

Janet turned to him and discovered him already looking at her. The intensity in his eyes captured hers and held them. She was aware then of a change in the nature of the looks they were exchanging, a twist in the type of communication passing between them that made the warm, humid air seem too heavy for breathing.

"Do you know what it does to me to look at those little bows on your shoulders?" he asked.

She shook her heat mutely, while her face grew warm and her chest felt heavy when she breathed.

"To know that one quick jerk would release them?" he continued. "To imagine what it would be like to kiss your bare shoulders and peel that dress down to your waist and see your breasts, touch them? I know what they look like, Janet, what they'd feel like. I've seen you with that wet swimsuit clinging to your nipples. But knowing just makes me crazier, like knowing what something tastes like makes you hungrier for it."

"Stephen," she whispered hoarsely, unsure whether it was a question or a plea or a simple confirmation that she was aware of who was there, talking to her that way. Aware? Every nerve ending in her body was aroused, alert, expectant.

With a growl of frustration, Stephen grabbed her hand and pulled her along the front of the building, gathering speed as they moved. His cane beat a quickening tattoo on the wooden walkway.

He paused long enough to offer an absurd, "Excuse us," to a couple they nearly bowled off the walkway, then resumed the harried pace until they reached the end of the building, stepped off the walkway and rounded the corner. . . .

9

HE LED HER ALONG the side of the building, away from the courtyard lights until they were deep in shadow, then stopped so abruptly Janet bumped into his chest as he spun to face her. Twisting, he turned her so that her back was to the building. His cane hit the building with a thud as he put his hands on either side of her, loosely trapping her between the building and his body.

He stared down at her, studying the way the pale light played on her features in the near darkness, then lifted his right hand to caress her face. He spoke with an unsettling intensity. "You're not a bimbo to me, Janet."

Before she could form a reply, he bent and kissed her hard on the mouth, urgently but briefly, before drawing away from her to rasp, "I want you, Janet. I want to make love to you, but not . . . not just because you're convenient. Do you understand what I'm saying? I want you, but it's not . . . casual. I've been holding back, trying to tell myself that it can't go beyond this island, this week, that it wouldn't be fair to ask you. . . ."

He was breathing heavily, as if he'd run a great distance. "But I'm going crazy wanting you, Janet. Even if it's just for now, while we're here together, let's share it. Let's share each other—" He groaned. "I sound like a sailor in port for a week. Is this making any sense?"

In response, Janet combed her fingers into his hair, covering his ears with her palms, and pulled his face down to hers. She initiated the kiss and at first controlled it, coaxing his lips apart with persistent flicks of her tongue, then invading his mouth with teasing thrusts that drew sensual groans from deep in his throat. Then he wedged her against the building with his body and, as his erection, discernibly hot and hard despite the barrier of their clothing, pressed unyieldingly, beseechingly, into her stomach, she realized that control was simply an illusion. She was no longer in control, she was afire with the need to feel that heat and hardness inside her.

It was a shock when Stephen pulled away from her. She sighed her frustration in a heavy moan that ended almost as a sob; her head drooped forward until her forehead rested against his breastbone. A tremor passed through his body, telling her that he was as stunned as she by the intensity of their mutual desire.

"Tonight," he said.

It was not a question, because she'd already given him the answer he sought. She nodded, silently acknowledging the fact of his statement with the brush of her forehead against his chest.

For a long time, neither of them moved. The noises of the evening—the chatter and laughter of the crowd swilling rum punch in the center court, the rustling of the trees in the breeze and the pipelike chirp of the Bajan crickets—drifted around them to remind them of where they were.

Gradually Stephen eased his body away from hers and slid his arms around her. This time the kiss, lingering but tender, was a promise. Janet was still loathe to move when it ended. "If I had my car I'd have you back to the Rockley so fast you'd have whiplash," Stephen said, and chortled dryly. "'A horse! A horse! My kingdom for a horse.'"

He released a haunted sigh and ran his fingers through his hair. "I wonder how fast they could get a taxi here."

"Maybe we should stay," Janet said meekly.

He looked at her as though she'd suggested they overthrow the free world.

"You've already paid for the tickets," she said. "And we're here."

Stephen indulged himself in a frown. "Stay we will, then," he said. With a sigh of resignation, he picked up his cane and raised his free arm in a sweeping gesture toward the courtyard. "Come on. I think we could use something cold to drink."

She walked ahead of him, and when she turned to enter the central yard, she was surprised to feel a slight pressure on her right shoulder. Stephen had grabbed one of the spaghetti straps, and her forward movement had untied the bow. She touched the straps that now hung over her breast and gave him a questioning look.

Smiling, he lifted the straps and retied the bow, pressing his finger into her shoulder as he held the knot in place while forming the loops. "Just practicing," he said.

They stopped at the drink table, then stood on the courtyard lawn sipping their island rum punch. Two waitresses in aprons and bandannas were circulating through the crowd with platters piled high with steaming hors d'oeuvres. One of them stopped to offer the golden-brown balls speared with toothpicks.

"What are these?" Janet asked as they each took one.

"Fish balls," the woman replied, and moved on.

"Interesting," Stephen said, biting into one of the crispy hors d'oeuvres, "but they don't taste like fish at all."

"Hush puppies!" Janet said, surprised.

"Beg your pardon?" Stephen said, finishing off his fish ball.

"Hush puppies. Fried corn bread. They eat them with fish in the American South. That's what these taste like, except a little . . . I don't know . . . the texture's a little different. Maybe they use a different grind of cornmeal."

As though he just couldn't keep his hands off her, Stephen draped his arms across her shoulders. "This is absurd, standing here talking about fish balls and something as ridiculous as hush-up dogs when I want you so badly."

"Hush puppies," Janet corrected hoarsely. The glint in his eye was doing crazy things to her throat.

"We should be kissing," he purred. "I should be untying these straps." He rolled the end of one of the straps between his thumb and forefinger, while the side of his hand rested against her shoulder blade.

"Stephen," she said. He was torturing her with the need he'd built in her.

"You're going to be sorry you insisted on staying," he whispered sensually, making it sound more like a promise than a threat.

"I didn't insist, I just said that since you'd already bought the tickets and we were here, we might as well..."

"You like?" a waitress said, presenting a platter laden with steaming hors d'oeuvres.

"Fish ball?" Stephen said, as though daring her to pluck fruit from a forbidden tree.

"Th-thank you," Janet told the waitress, taking a fish ball from the platter. Grinning, Stephen shook his head and waved the waitress on. Janet studied the fish ball on the end of the toothpick and, thinking of nothing else to do with it, popped it into her mouth. It stuck in her throat like a lump of peanut butter, and she swallowed a generous draft of rum punch to wash it down.

Stephen moved closer until his lips brushed her ear, "Careful on the rum, Janet. You wouldn't want to get tipsy. You might miss something."

Ordinarily Janet would have thought it was the alcohol making her warm. But she knew it wasn't the rum bringing color to her cheeks. It was anticipation, pure and simple.

She took another gulp of punch, grateful to feel a piece of ice flow into her mouth along with the rum-rich punch. She held it on her tongue a moment, savoring its coldness.

"They're serving," Stephen said, lifting his arm in a wide gesture toward the buffet tables. "Shall we?"

They found their assigned seats, left their drinks and his cane on the table and joined the line that had formed at the buffet. Although they scarcely spoke, Stephen managed to constantly remind Janet of his presence. His hand seemed to have found a permanent resting place on her shoulder near the straps of her dress, and his forefinger slid back and forth over her skin in a subtle movement that would have seemed mindless if he had not paused every so often and waited for her to turn her face to his expectantly. Then he would smile knowingly and continue the seemingly innocuous stroking.

The buffet was very similar to the one served at the Rockley: breaded fillet of flying fish, mashed pumpkin, rice and peas, breadfruit, roast chicken. Janet dutifully put out her plate and allowed the servers to pile on the island specialties, but she found she had little appetite—at least for flying fish and pumpkin—once they returned to the table.

The folding chairs were placed so close together that Stephen's arm crushed against hers, and under the table, his muscled thigh aligned with hers. The word he'd rasped—*tonight*—echoed again and again in her mind. Within hours they would be lovers, and it was for that intimacy she hungered, not for the hearty foods of the island. Each touch, each whiff of his cologne, each meaningful look they exchanged became an appetizer that whetted her hunger.

The show they'd come to see should have been preemptive. Women in colorful full skirts and cotton lace petticoats and men in white pants and shirts and brilliantly colored sashes danced to the beat of drums, acting out, through the universal language of dance, scenes from the island's history.

But every scene dealt in some way with love and lovers. Sailor's women waited on and watched for ships, soldier's women waited and watched for their men. Ill-fated love, a lover's betrayal, unrequited love were all played out in folkloric ballet.

The drums—snare, bass and kettle—throbbed with a primal beat that mimicked the rhythms of life—of beating hearts and the frenzied, escalating cadence of the act of procreation.

The drumbeats reverberated through the tropic night, while dancers whirled and twirled across the stage, the light-colored pads of their bare feet flashing in brilliant contrast to their dark bronze or ebony skins, with an effect no costume designer could recreate with fabric or paint.

The women flitted and flirted and undulated seductively, eternal coquettes, while the men gyrated, leaped and swiveled their hips with strength and prowess and all the strutting pride of peacocks spreading and shaking their feathers to impress the female of the species.

The air was heavy with sensuality, pregnant with sexual suggestion. Beside her, Stephen was warm, his cologne was expensive, and when he touched her, Janet felt more alive and female than she'd ever felt in her life. Tonight he'd become her lover. *Tonight.*

Stephen slid his hand under her braids to massage her neck. He gathered a handful of braids and weighed them in his palm, then closed his hand around them and pulled slightly until she turned her face away from the dancers and looked at him, into the desire in his eyes. One thought skittered back and forth between them like an arcing electrical spark: *tonight.*

The frenzied beating of the drums crescendoed and then faded into a shattering silence. The stage lights went down, the lights in the yard went up, and the applause of the audience exploded into the silence. *Intermission.*

"I'll go for drinks," Stephen said. "With or without the rum?"

"Without," Janet said, wondering how he could look so calm when she felt the complete opposite.

The iced tropical fruit punch he brought back wet the throat and quenched thirst, but it couldn't quell the inferno of anticipation burning inside a woman about to take a lover. Janet thought again of the way she'd joked with her friends at work about meeting a gorgeous hunk and having a wild affair. Had that really been less than a week ago, when she'd spoken with such bravado about an island lover?

A wave of panic seized her. What did she know about the protocol of a wild vacation affair? She wasn't prepared for this. She hadn't even brought... Her eyes widened.

Stephen sensed her change of mood. "Janet?"

"Come with me," she said, grabbing his hand as she almost knocked her chair over in her haste to leave the table.

"What is—"

"We've got to talk," she whispered urgently.

They stopped in a shadowy corner of the patio beyond the now deserted buffet serving tables. The concern showed in Stephen's eyes as he asked, "What is it, Janet?"

"I don't . . . I didn't bring . . . I joked with Trudy about having an affair but . . ." She sighed like a balloon deflating. "I didn't bring any . . . you know."

"Condoms?"

"I never thought . . . I mean, I thought that if . . . that there would be drugstores."

Stephen was careful to wrap his arms around her reassuringly *before* he succumbed to laughter. "You are so charming, Janet. It's all right. There's no problem."

Her head flew up so she could see his face. "You have one?"

He bent and kissed the tip of her nose. "A baker's dozen, if you count the one in my wallet."

She sighed. "I'm glad. I—"

He cut off the rest of the sentence by swallowing it in a kiss. She clung to him as he tried to draw away.

"The show's starting again," he murmured.

"Who cares?" she asked, capturing his face in her hands and pulling it back to hers.

The show had indeed started by the time they returned to their seats. It was an extension of the first half, with the dances more intricate, the leaps and other movements of the dancers more daring. One scenario pitted two young men in competition for a young girl's attention. They took turns dancing for her in an effort to impress her with their strength and virility.

Each new segment was more explicit, as the drums beat faster and faster and the men's strutting and gyrating became frenzied and blatantly sexual. The male dancers were fit and lean, with powerful muscles that strained against the cloth of their costumes. But it was not the dancers themselves that affected Janet, it was the primal theme of the dance, the sexual suggestion in the escalating drumbeats that vibrated through the night air.

She felt the tension all through her body. *Tonight.* Her scalp tingled with it, and there was a tautness in her middle that could be uncoiled only one way. Stephen was touching her, drawing circles on her skin with his forefinger, rubbing his thumb along the side of her neck, toying with her braids.

She gasped when he pushed her hair to one side and pressed a kiss on her nape, then flicked his tongue across that sensitive patch of skin. She wanted more than anything in the world to turn around and get lost in the strength of his arms, to let the dark island night swallow them while they made love.

The show ended with a finale of bright color and daring leaps. Janet and Stephen, walking arm in arm, were the first to reach the bus. They slid into the very last seat, which afforded them a modicum of privacy while they waited for the other passengers. Nearly half an hour crawled by, minute by interminable minute, before the bus driver closed the doors and ground the bus's engine to life.

With the interior lights doused, the bus was dark—dark enough for Stephen to slide his arm around Janet and for Janet to rest her head in the crook of his shoulder. He used his free hand to play with the straps of her dress while he launched a campaign of subtle sensuous torture.

"I can hardly wait to untie these straps," he whispered. "Are you wearing anything under that top?"

"Only—" she rasped.

But he shushed her with, "Don't tell me. I want to find out on my own." He ran his finger along the top edge of the bodice, letting her know how easy it would be for him to peel the garment away.

He kissed the curve of her shoulder and told her how sweet she was, then nipped the lobe of her ear, blew into it gently and promised, "I'm going to devour you."

The bus made stop after stop, letting passengers file out, until finally they reached the Rockley and it was Janet and Stephen's turn to get off. Wordlessly they crossed the street and followed the path along the golf course.

There was an oak tree near the edge of the course, huge, gnarled and venerable, silhouetted in the moonlight. Stephen led her under its branches, deep into shadow, and kissed her with an urgency that made her weak-kneed and breathless. Then he took off again, walking quickly, oblivious to his limp, pulling her along with him.

His face was grin with determination. He didn't pause to ask, "My place or yours?" but let her straight to his bungalow and ushered her directly into the bedroom, where an air conditioner in the window produced what felt like a near-arctic atmosphere in contrast to the heat that had accumulated in the living area of the closed bungalow.

"Finally," he said, drawing her into his arms. His mouth fused with hers in a plundering kiss of possession. His arms tightened around her, crushing her body into a startling intimacy with his.

Janet couldn't think anymore; his stark virility stole away all logic, leaving only sensual perception. She tugged the tail of his shirt free of his pants and slid her hands inside, running her palms over the hard, smooth sinews of his back.

Mouth still fused with hers, Stephen pulled on the spaghetti straps on her left shoulder, blindly wrestling them until the bow was untied and then brushing them aside impatiently. Reaching his arm around her, he did the same thing on the other shoulder, working from the back.

With a sensual growl, he tore his mouth from hers. She was breathing heavily, and the quivering motion of her chest drew his gaze. The way he looked at her, at the skin above the bodice of her dress, caused her breath to catch. She watched, fascinated, as he raised his hand and spread it over her left breast, noticed with an odd awareness of detail how the color of his skin contrasted with the pastel blue of her dress. She released the air she'd been holding in her lungs when he pressed his palm into her nipple and closed his fingers slightly, molding them around the fullness of her breast. Her own hands convulsed into fists, squeezing the hard muscles of his back.

The beads on her braids clicked as she threw her head back, and a sensual purr slid from her throat as she felt his forefinger slide inside the bodice and trace the lace edge of her dress from side to side.

"Look at me, Janet," he said, the soft French inflection of his speech turning the order and her name into an endearment.

Slowly her eyes found his and followed his gaze to her chest.

She could feel the intensity with which he stared at the lace-edged bodice; her entire body tautened in response to it. And then, with a swiftness that was almost violent, he thrust his finger down, forcing the bodice along with it. He laughed softly at the lace bandeau bra that stretched over her breasts, not in amusement, but in the power of new knowledge of her intimate secrets. The open pattern of the lace hid very little. Her nipples were erect, her areolae noticeably darker than the surrounding skin.

With another deliberate movement, he slid his finger between her breasts, behind the bandeau, and eased the lace down. Janet followed his gaze to the flesh he'd just bared, and then looked at his face and was stunned by the degree of concentration she saw there. She was warm suddenly; heat was suffusing her body from a source buried deep inside her.

She shoved his shirt up, bunching it under his arms. For several seconds she stared at his chest, nothing the hard swells of muscle, the brown male nipples, the sprinkling of brown hair. With a pained sigh, she leaned forward, pressing her soft, full breasts against that hard wall of male muscle.

Stephen fought the shirt over his head and flung it aside, then wrapped his arms around her. He concentrated now on the shoulders that had tantalized him all evening and the sweet junction of her neck to those shoulders. He tasted it with his tongue and found it not sweet but exotically delicious, as only a woman could taste. Desperate to get even closer to her, he cupped her buttocks and, lifting, pulled her up into his hardness.

Her skirt slipped slightly under his open hand, and it suddenly seemed to be an enemy force, barring them from the contact he so desperately needed. He groped at it, gathering it into his hands, until he came to the hem and, with an impatient flip of his wrists, worked his hands under the edge. As he spread his fingers over the swell of her buttocks, only a wisp of satin blocked his hands from the feel of her skin. Then, in the frenzy of a man close to fulfillment, he breached that frail barricade of elastic and satin. Janet whimpered, echoing his urgent need.

"The bed," he said. Without letting go of her, he backed her to the low bed and fell onto it, bringing her down beside him. Shoving her skirt up around her waist, he clasped the side of her panties and yanked them over her legs. Janet cooperated, kicking free of them when they reached her ankles and tossing her sandals off at the same time.

Once again Stephen's eyes feasted on the beauty of her body. The expression on his face as he gazed down at her made Janet warmer still. The thought flitted through her mind that she should be embarrassed, but she felt honored that a man would look at her with such undisguised desire and found that his desire excited her.

Almost reverently he touched her stomach, letting his hand rest there lightly for a few seconds before moving it lower. The heel of his hand and then his fingertips brushed over the mound between her legs.

Arching against him, seeking that wondrous friction that would assuage the need he sent raging through her, she cried out. "Kiss me," she said, holding up her arms, and he moved his body over hers, letting her arms enfold him while he obliged her with the kiss she'd asked for. The weight of his chest crushed into her breasts, and his erection, bulging against the zipper of his pants, throbbed against her.

He arched, thrusting toward her, then groaned in frustration at the barriers between them. Rolling away from her, he tore at the belt and waistband of his pants, fumbling in his urgency, but managed to shove them down his legs, underwear and all. They caught on his injured leg, and he cursed violently but persisted until he had his shoes and pants off.

He stretched out next to her again. Their eyes met, and Janet saw tenderness there as well as desire. As if to confirm what she'd seen, he kissed her with heartrending gentleness. But the gentleness gave way to urgency as his hand found her breast. He slid his healthy leg over hers, insinuating his thigh between hers. He groaned into her mouth and pushed his leg further, bringing himself closer still.

"I've got to get inside you," he rasped.

She twisted onto her side, so that his erection brushed her mound, this time without the barrier of clothing.

He grated out an expletive and leaped away from her, yelping as his weight shifted uncomfortably onto his sore leg.

"Stephen?"

"I damned near forgot," he said, grabbing his pants and digging for his wallet. "You should have reminded me."

"I damned near forgot, too," she said breathlessly. "And I'm not . . . up on the etiquette."

He looked down at her, exposed and vulnerable with her skirt around her waist and her bodice pushed down. She wasn't up on the etiquette. She hadn't been prepared. *Congratulations, Dumont, you win the award for insensitivity.*

He sat on the edge of the bed next to her and pushed her braids away from her face, fanning them out on the pillow. "How does this dress come off? Up over your head or . . ."

"Up would be easier," she said, pulling herself into a sitting position.

He gathered the dress into his hands and guided it over her head and arms, then touched the lace bandeau that had crawled to her waist. "And this?"

"Same way."

It was trickier because it was tight. He was careful, trying to prevent it from pinching her breasts by stretching it apart with his hands as it passed over their fullness.

Janet captured his face in her hands. "Do you know how erotic it is, having you undress me this way?"

"Trust me, Janet, I know."

"Kiss me."

"I assure you, I intend to do more than that." He studied the tiny scrap of lace after it had cleared her hands. "What a ridiculous garment!"

Janet snatched the bra from him and tossed it across the room, then caught his face in her hands again. "Kiss me."

Stephen obliged with a quick brush of his lips over hers, but when he went to draw away, she trapped him by sliding her arms around his neck. "Properly."

"There is no way to kiss a naked woman *properly*," he said. "If I start kissing you in earnest, we're going to be right back where we were when I got up to dig around in my billfold."

His gaze had drifted to her breasts, and he groaned as he gently pushed her arms from around his neck. "Safe sex is the pits, do you know that?"

He'd found the condom in his billfold earlier and laid the foil pouch on the bedside table. Now he opened it. Janet watched, fascinated, while he positioned the condom and began unrolling it over his erection. He caught her watching and smiled self-consciously.

"You're beautiful," she said. "A beautiful man. Do you need help?"

"I just need *you* after I get the damned thing on." He smiled, thinking how pretty she was. "I don't seem to be having any problem staying ready."

"I don't, either," she said, and surprised them both by reaching out to cup him with her fingertips.

Stephen repeated the expletive he'd said earlier, explosively this time, and rolled over abruptly, trapping her under him. "Now we kiss," he said. "Properly, improperly and any other damned way we please."

And kiss they did—properly, improperly, *quite* improperly. Briefly, lingeringly, probingly. Slowly, urgently, sweetly. Hotly, frenziedly, loving. By the time Janet whispered, "Now, Stephen," all Stephen could say was, "Yes. Yes," with the same breathless urgency.

He invaded her warm, wet velvet softness with a slow persistent thrust. Several timeless seconds passed as they adjusted to the most intimate caress of one body by another, before Stephen moved gently, stroking, and Janet responded with a complementary motion. They were lost then, to everything but each other and the frantic need driving them to fulfillment.

Janet was the first to reach that sensual peak. "Hold me," she said, arching against him. "Please. Hold me."

She hugged him with surprising strength. Stephen dropped gentle kisses over her face. "So sweet," he whispered. "Sweet, sweet Janet."

Slowly she relaxed, and her breathing eased toward normalcy. "You," she said, and he began moving inside her again, gently at first and then faster, as her hands played over his back, until at last his own uncoiling began. She soothed him as he'd soothed her, stroking his hair and kissing his temple while he lay atop her, weak with satisfaction.

At last he sighed, gingerly rolled away from her, and sat up, dropping his feet to the floor. "Safe sex is the pits," he said again, and walked out of the room.

Minutes later he returned and paused just inside the door to look at Janet, who was lying with the sheet pulled up under her arms. The angle at which she lay left her back exposed to below the waist.

He walked to the bed with a very vivid appreciation of what a lucky man he was. Without getting under the sheets, he stretched out beside her and put his hand on her shoulder and slid it down her arm before dancing his fingertips across her smooth back. She sighed languidly, a sigh of pure pleasure, as smug as a tomcat's purr.

"It was very special for me, Janet," he said.

She rolled over. She was smiling. "I love the way you say my name. Your accent softens it."

Stephen grinned. "What accent?"

"Your French accent, silly. Most people say, Jan-it. Like the two words pushed together, *Jan* and *it*."

"And how do I say it so differently?"

"You say Jan-eet. Like *Jan, eat*, only softer."

"Maybe it's the way I'm feeling when I say it, instead of the accent so much."

Janet pushed up on one elbow so that they were almost nose to nose. "How are you feeling when you say it?"

"Like you are a very special woman."

She slinked down, letting her head sink into the pillow next to his. "You make me feel that way when you say it."

They were quiet a moment. Pensive. Content. Their faces were scarcely an inch apart on the pillow. Stephen pushed a braid away from her cheek and said, "Your hair smells good, Janet."

"But?" she asked, reading the hesitation in his speech.

"But I would very much like to be able to comb my fingers through it, and kiss you without making it click."

"Long and loose," Janet said, amused at the predictability of it.

He took it for a question. "Yes." After a pause, he said, "Do you remember what I said when you asked what I thought of it?"

"That you'd like to be the one to take it out?"

"I would still like that pleasure."

"Start with the ones on the bottom and work up," she said.

"You don't mind, after you had someone do this?"

"I think it would be difficult to sleep on the beads," she said.

"I would risk the threat to my shoulder if you would stay with me tonight."

She smiled at him, a smile of acquiescence. "But there's no danger. You're going to unbraid it, aren't you?"

"Braid by braid."

Minutes later she was laying with her back to him while he uncurled the foil, removed the beads and combed out the braids with his fingers. It had taken him a few tries to perfect the technique of starting at the ends and working slowly upward, undoing it twist by twist. But with benefit of practice, he worked with the dexterity of a surgeon. The effect of his ministrations was far from clinical, however.

The pressure of his fingers combing through her hair, the massage of his fingertips when they worked their way to her scalp and the kiss he dropped onto her nape, shoulder or spine after finishing each braid put her in a state of sensual bliss.

It was divine, lying there, having a man devote his undivided attention to her, using his strong hands in such a gentle way. The intimacy of it lulled her. She was disinclined to move a single muscle other than those required to breathe and felt the sublime privilege of knowing no one expected her to.

"Your hair is very fluffy now," Stephen said.

"Braids always make hair curly." Several lazy minutes passed, undisturbed except for the period thunk of a bead being dropped into the ashtray on the bedside table before Janet said, "Your sisters have French names."

"And Stephen is not French, and you want to know how I got it."

"Um," Janet agreed. The word sounded like a sigh.

"I was named for my father's ski coach. He was a friend to my father, as well as his coach."

"He must have been honored to have a namesake."

"He was like a grandfather to me. He told me stories about my father. About going to the Olympics and all the mischief the skiers got into, and how proud everyone was when my father won his medals." He tossed another bead into the ashtray and sighed before combing through the braid he'd just freed. "That's all I remember about him. He died when I was seven."

He loosened the braid and several more, then pulled her hair back and kissed her behind the ear. "Turn your head so I can get to the other side."

"What was it like growing up with a famous father?" she asked. Her face was turned toward him now.

"I never gave it much thought. He was my father, and he was famous. It seemed perfectly normal to me, because it was always so. My father was a charismatic man, always surrounded by people. They adored him for his energy and his talent, and I adored him for all the same qualities."

He paused pensively. "He taught me to ski almost as soon as I could walk. I used to watch him move on the snow, so graceful, and be awed by him. Everything he could teach me, I learned, but for me, it was mostly skill. My talent was only slightly above average. But him—skill simply augmented great talent. He was destined to win Olympic gold, and I was lucky to take one Canadian National."

He held a half-unbraided strand of hair in his hands. "I would not have won it if another skier had not been injured the week of the competition. I did not want to win the championship that way. It's almost as though I cheated a friend, who was a better skier."

"That's the nature of competitive athletics, isn't it? The medal goes to the best performance at a particular moment on a particular day. Don't athletes take it for granted they are vulnerable to injuries, and that's part of the challenge of competition?"

A muscle flexed in Stephen's cheek as he considered the question. His seriousness surprised Janet, because she had meant the question to be largely rhetorical.

"I suppose," he said, and paused. "Intellectually, I suppose that's true, although... I don't think anyone really expects it to happen to them. I never thought... My father skied all his life, with nothing more than an occasional pulled muscle. I must have felt that I shared his invincibility."

"Invincibility, or luck."

Stephen looked at her face then, and she sensed that he was returning to her mentally after a period of deep introspection. "Mostly luck, I suppose, although I never realized it before. He seemed, and still seems, invincible."

"Are you still close?"

"Yes. He's never lost that charismatic energy. Even if he weren't my father, I would admire him, the way so many do."

"He had you late in life."

Stephen smiled. "He married late, when he was forty. He was a notorious playboy—world famous, in fact, considered to be a real catch. The marriage generated a lot of excitement and speculation. She was so much younger and so different from the jet-setters he normally dated."

"How did they meet?"

"She came to the Chalet Dumont to audition for a job, and my father fell madly in love with her. They were married within weeks."

Janet snuggled her cheek against the pillow and sighed. "That's very romantic."

Stephen tossed a bead into the ashtray, then dipped to kiss the cheek exposed to him. "Yes. I always marveled that it could happen, it seems so . . . absurd, that after all those women, he could see one shy piano player and, pow! love at first sight. Yet thirty-five years later, they are still devoted to one another. No one can doubt that bond. It is not merely that they have become a habit to each other."

"My parents were close, too. It was hard for my mother after he died, especially since it was... unexpected. I think moving was good for her. She's been forced to establish new routines. The change made letting go easier."

"When did he die?"

"Three years ago," Janet said softly. "He was clearing the driveway and . . . he had a heart attack. It was very quick."

"While shoveling snow."

"He'd had high blood pressure for several years, and there were a number of warning signs, although he—we all—failed to see them."

"But it happened in the snow."

She closed her eyes and exhaled heavily. "Yes."

"I'm sorry, Janet."

"Don't be." She opened her eyes, and he could see the pain remembering her father's death brought to her. "It was inevitable. It could have happened just as easily in the summer while he was mowing grass."

Combing his fingers into the section of hair he'd finished unbraiding, he pulled it away from her face. His thumb caressed her cheek as he lowered his mouth to hers for a consoling kiss.

After drawing away, he smiled down at her. "Just a few more to go, here on top." A minute or so later he was running his fingers all through her hair, fluffing it.

"It's all kinky, isn't it?" Janet asked, not liking the amused grin settling on his face. "It's all kinky and I look ridiculous." She tugged the sheet over her head and heard his grin escalate into full laughter. "I wanted to look like Bo Derek, and I probably look like a French poodle with his tail in a light socket."

Stephen ran his hand back and forth over the sheet spread tautly over her body, pausing on the feminine swell of her buttocks before smacking it firmly. Janet gasped and jerked into a sitting position, shoving the sheet out of the way, only to have Stephen laugh triumphantly. "I thought that would get your attention."

The indignant protest on the tip of her tongue never found voice, because his mouth fused over hers. His fingers caressed her scalp as he eased her back down onto the bed. She realized, without regret, that the sheet had slipped down to her waist as Stephen's chest pressed deliciously against her naked breasts. He tore his mouth off hers to kiss her cheek, the line of her jaw and, finally, her neck.

"You don't look at all like a poodle," he whispered.

His voice, husky with arousal, had an aphrodisiac effect. With open hands, she explored his muscled shoulders, then his spine, following it to the small of his back. She stroked him there, with butterfly landings of her fingertips.

"Your hair is soft, Janet. It smells so good. And you are beautiful." He trailed kisses from her neck down to her breastbone and paused there, testing the taste of her skin with his tongue. He draped his leg, knee bent, over hers; the heat of his thighs was wildly erotic as it radiated through the sheet. His erection pulsed and grew, straining to be readmitted to that warm, private place inside her.

As he kissed her, the fresh growth of beard gently chafed her breasts, scarcely more abrasive than the rub of his chest hair, but infinitely more arousing. Cheek against her breastbone, he traced the outside edge of her areola with his forefinger and watched her nipple tauten. Then, smiling against that soft, yielding mound of female flesh, he turned his head and took it into his mouth. He sucked on it, roughed it with his tongue, drew again, urging a sigh from her as she wriggled involuntarily beneath him. She shifted accommodatingly when he moved to the other breast to give it the same loving attention.

He slid his hand under the sheet and splayed it over her ribs before then moving it over and down. For several seconds he held it over her stomach, palm over her navel while he continued kissing and kneading her breast. Then he kissed his way to her navel and dipped his tongue into that depression while the heel of his hand brushed over the sensitive area at the juncture of her thighs.

She arched against him, and he raised his head to hers again to whisper into her ear, "I want you again, Janet. Are you ready for me?" As he asked that question, his finger probed inside her for the answer and found the moist, unmistakable proof that she was. He swallowed her gasp at the unexpected, glorious invasion in a greedy kiss, and when at last he tore his lips from hers, she groaned sensuously in protest.

"Time for responsibility," he said soothingly, nibbling at her cheek. "What I need is in the bathroom."

She nodded, but her arms tightened around his neck. "Safe sex is the pits," she said breathlessly.

10

JANET WONDERED what was keeping Stephen. It seemed to her he'd been gone for a very long time, but she supposed that her perception of time was warped by impatience.

With a sigh, she patted her hair with her hands, well remembering the feel of Stephen's fingers combing through the braids and caressing her scalp. To her own analytical fingers, her hair felt flyaway as dandelion fluff. It must be standing out four inches from her head. It was too soft for her to gauge whether it was curly or frizzy or merely crimped, but she'd lay odds that Stephen had told a gracious lie when he said she didn't look like a poodle.

She was still tingling from his touch; her breasts felt slightly heavy, the area between her legs hot and moist and yearning.

What was taking him so long?

On impulse, she crawled out of bed. Several shirts were hanging in the closet and she pulled on one, suddenly shy about going to him totally exposed, although she wasn't intimidated enough to bother buttoning the buttons. The bathroom door was ajar, and she could see his reflection in the mirror above the sink. Confident that she wasn't interrupting any specific biological function better left uninterrupted, she knocked gently on the door and pushed it open.

"Janet!" he said, with the mien of a person unpleasantly surprised.

"I hope you don't mind my borrowing your shirt. I was lonely, and I thought I'd see how ridiculous my hair really. . ."

Her voice abandoned her as she caught sight of the reason he'd decided to hole up in the bathroom. She drew in a gulp of air with a wheezing sound while her hand flew to her mouth in consternation.

Stephen's mouth hardened into a menacing frown, and his face turned a vivid shade of humiliated red. "I'm going to *kill* Brigitte."

"It's striped," Janet said, eyes fixed on his rubber-sheathed penis.

"They were supposed to be 'designer,' but I thought it would just be colors."

"It's *green,*" Janet said. "It's striped, and it's green."

"It's called Jungle Stalker. It sounded less innocuous than Banana Banger or Passionate Pimento, but—" his eyes leveled on her threateningly "—laugh, and so help me. . ."

But he'd known when he said it that she was going to laugh; he could hear it building up, gurgling in her throat just begging to be let out. And laugh she did. "I'm s-sorry," she said, through erupting gales. "It's just so unexpected."

Grabbing her shoulders, he said, "It'll get the job done." He pulled her into his arms in a crushing hug and bent to kiss her. But as his lips touched hers, she fell victim to a wave of giggles.

"What now?" he growled.

"It looks gangrenous," she wheezed. "You didn't get it caught in your zipper, did you?"

Experience with his sisters had taught Stephen that with females, giggles were far more formidable to deal with than tears—and must be dealt with sternly. "Janet!" he snapped.

The harshness in his voice caused her to choke back her laughter, but it was only a brief respite. Once the shock of the command wore off, the thunderous, brooding expression on his face suddenly struck her as hilarious, and she was overcome by a fresh eruption of giggles.

"Women are the most trying creatures on the face of the earth!" Stephen grumbled. And then, totally exasperated, he almost shouted, "For pity's sake, Janet, quit laughing at me. I might lose it forever, and never be able to—"

"It's not you," she said, straining the words through the incipient giggles. "It's really not . . . it's . . . just . . . so . . . *green*."

"You're hysterical," Stephen said matter-of-factly.

Lowering her voice an octave and affecting the sound track of a B-grade horror movie promo, she said, "It's the Jungle Stalker from the Black Lagoon!" and succumbed to a fresh wave of laughter.

With a long growl of utter exasperation, Stephen lunged for her, bending to position his shoulder in the general vicinity of her belly button. He crossed his arms behind her knees and, with a grunt of strain, lifted her straight off the floor.

"Stephen!" Janet cried, shocked out of her laughter. "Stephen! Put me down!"

"I'll show you what happens to hysterical women!"

"Your leg," she said. "You shouldn't be—"

"Men with green stalks can do anything," he said expansively. "And quit wiggling." He gave her backside a generous swat for emphasis.

He struggled with the bedroom door and won, managing to get Janet through it without inflicting a concussion, then kicked it closed behind them. He tossed Janet onto the bed and then fell atop her, trapping her between his body and the mattress.

"You're wrinkling your shirt," she said.

"My shirt be damned!" he said, and kissed her senseless. He was straddling her, his erection pressed above the hollow between her thighs. His voice was husky and sensual. "It doesn't matter so much now that it's green with stripes, does it?"

He kissed her again, ruthlessly probing her mouth with his tongue. She was breathless when he lifted his mouth from hers to observe, "You're not laughing anymore."

"Is this called sweeping a woman off her feet?" she asked, chest heaving.

Stephen was breathing rapidly, as well. Cupping her buttocks in his hands, he lifted her slightly and thrust into her moist, waiting softness. A sensual growl rose in his throat as he watched and felt her body absorb his

"It's called . . . destiny," he rasped, and began stroking inside her.

A long time later, they lay together, contented and near sleep, in the double bed. His arm was around Janet's neck, and her cheek rested on his chest. Her leg, bent at the knee, was draped over his thighs, a welcome, pleasurable weight.

Sighing, Janet snuggled a little closer and said his name.

"Hmm?" he answered lazily.

"Why do you want to kill Brigitte?"

STEPHEN AWOKE in an empty bed, and it took him a few seconds to miss Janet. Then the sensual reminders of her that lingered in the bed—the scent of her hair clinging to the pillow, the warmth of the sheet where she'd lain—stirred memories of the night before, and with them, memories of the woman with whom he'd shared such pleasure. Alert now, he was relieved to hear water running in the bathroom, evidence that she was still in the bungalow.

In a few minutes, the hinges on the bathroom door squeaked, and seconds later he heard the knob of the bedroom door being turned. He closed his eyes, playing possum, then watched with surreptitious looks as she tiptoed around, gathering her clothes and trying to be quiet. She was still wearing his shirt, the one she'd slept in. Neither of them had ever gotten around to buttoning it, so as she moved, he caught tantalizing glimpses of her breasts, the gentle curve of her tummy, the triangle of hair at the juncture of her legs.

Her lace bandeau bra still lay on the floor in the corner of the room where she'd tossed it. She stooped to pick it up, then held it in her hand. The smile that softened her face reflected some of the same wonder he felt over their lovemaking, and he suddenly felt voyeuristic observing her without her knowledge.

"You aren't thinking of putting that on and leaving me, are you?" he asked.

Startled, she gasped and, in a reflexive reaction, pulled the sides of the shirt together over her breasts. "Stephen!" Then, recovering she said, "I didn't mean to wake you."

"The question was," he said, "were you planning on leaving?"

Guilt crossed over her face. "I was going to leave you a note."

He hated the sudden morning-after awkwardness between them. They'd been too close for this cloying self-consciousness. "Why don't you tell me what it was going to say."

She sat down on the edge of the bed, less tense now that they were talking. "I'm booked on a tour this morning, and I've got to wash my hair and get dressed."

He reached for her hand and threaded his fingers through hers. The gesture of a lover. "Skip the tour," he said. "Spend the day with me."

Conflicting emotions showed in her eyes. "I've already made reservations."

He didn't argue, but his silence was eloquent, as was the hard line of displeasure around his mouth.

"This tour doesn't run every day; I might not be able to get on another one before I leave."

His silence unnerved her, making her defensive.

"I don't do a lot of world traveling. I want to see the island," she said, irritated that she felt compelled to explain. For good measure, she added, "I cater to tourists all the time. I want to *be* one for a change."

"What time must you meet the tour?"

"Seven forty-five."

"And what time is it now?"

"Just after six."

He grinned at her, that sexy, seductive grin that made wonderful things happen in the pit of her stomach. "How long will it take you to get ready?"

"An hour."

Still grinning seductively, he pulled her hand to his lips and kissed the top of it, then turned it over and did the same to the underside of her wrist. "A whole hour?"

"Forty-five minutes," she amended.

The grin became a smile, wide, radiant, triumphant. "Which leaves us time—" he kissed his way up her arm, pulling her closer to him and coaxing her down on the bed "—to say good morning."

This time their lovemaking was gentle and quite thorough. By the time Stephen walked Janet to her bungalow, she was questioning her decision to take the tour instead of spending the day with Stephen. Logic told her that she couldn't afford to pay for the tour and not take it; that she was on a vacation of a lifetime and shouldn't miss out on seeing Barbados when she had the chance; that Stephen, who obviously traveled much more than she, was selfish in asking her to give up the tour.

But she couldn't concentrate on logic when Stephen kissed her gently and told her how much he'd enjoyed being with her and made her promise to have dinner with him. He was too virile, too *tangible* to ignore when his arms were around her and his body was pressing warmly against hers.

"I'll see you tonight," he said.

The temptation was there to call him back as she watched him walk away. Anyone could go to Barbados and see turquoise water, tropical vegetation, caves and old churches; how many met a man like Stephen Dumont?

Then reason prevailed and, begrudging its intrusion, Janet entered her bungalow to shower and dress for the tour.

Half an hour later she studied her reflection in the mirror and wondered if it was her time at the beach or her time in Stephen Dumont's bed that had given her skin such a healthy glow. She felt rather conspicuous after the night she'd just spent making love, as though people would look at her and think, "There's a woman who's been loved thoroughly and well, who feels desirable, who's suddenly more aware than usual of her womanhood and celebrating it."

She felt a slight residual soreness between her legs as she walked, but she didn't mind the discomfort of excess. Too much of a good thing could be vexing, but it would seem petty to resent the effects of too much of a *great* thing!

A number of Rockley guests were milling in the central lobby, all clustered into couples or family units. It was easy to distinguish between the beach crowd, who wore swimsuits and fat-soled sandals with ribbon straps, and the tour crowd, in cotton shorts and shirts and flat walking shoes.

The beach crowd cleared out swiftly upon arrival of the beach shuttle. Janet surveyed her remaining fellow tourists with an evaluative eye and suffered a sinking feeling that she would most likely wind up being paired in a double seat with some elderly woman who had the misfortune of being the only other unaccompanied member of the tour. For this she had given up a day with Stephen Dumont?

Then a tap on her shoulder and a familiar voice asking, "Hey, beautiful, sitting with anybody special?" caused her to jerk her head around to look squarely into the face of the man about whom she'd been daydreaming.

"Stephen, what—?"

"You didn't think I'd let you get away so easily if I wasn't already booked into this tour?"

"Already?"

"Uh-huh. Yesterday. *I* was going to play hooky and spend the day with you, but when you insisted on coming, I decided to surprise you." He smiled that charming, naughty, little-boy smile. "You don't mind, do you?"

Mind? When they had the entire day stretching before them filled with turquoise water, caves and old churches? She could only shake her head to indicate that she didn't mind, while hoping that the involuntary smile forming on her mouth didn't make her look like a love-struck moose.

The tour bus arrived promptly at the appointed time, and they were surprised to discover rain clouds gathering in the sky when they went outside to board. John, their driver, a middle-aged man in his early fifties, whose rugged features and ruddy complexion suggested that he'd be as much at home in a barroom brawl as a tour bus, assured them the clouds probably would generate only a brief shower then dissipate.

His prediction proved true. It poured rain as the bus headed up Barbados's major coastal highway, but the shower lasted only minutes and left in its wake a wide, vivid rainbow that seemed to jut out of the sea. It hung above the turquoise water, a shimmering effervescence of colors—a mirror reflection of Janet's mood. "It's magnificent!" she said, awed.

Stephen, leaning close to her to peer through the window, put a caressing hand on her shoulder. They watched until the highway angled inland and they could no longer see the rainbow.

The vegetation along the roadway grew lush. As they approached the city of Holetown, John, speaking into a microphone with an accent more British than Bajan, told them about the expensive real estate between the highway and the sea: multimillion-dollar homes and the world-famous Sandy Lane hotel, playground of movie stars, rock legends, royalty and world leaders.

Next they passed through Speightstown in St. Peter, where Bajans scurried from shop to shop, taking care of the business of their daily lives. The two-story shops with Georgian-style balconies that lined the narrow city streets reminded Janet of the New Orleans French Quarter.

Another few miles up the road, in St. Lucy Parish, picturesque cottages dotted the landscape. Built of wood and often roofed with corrugated tin, the cubelike houses were painted bright colors, with contrasting trim at the windows and doors.

"These are the famous chattel houses," John told them. "After slavery was abolished in the mid-nineteenth century, many of the former slaves became indentured servants. They lived on the plantation where they worked, but the land on which they lived was rented from their landlord. So they developed a method of constructing houses that could be dismantled and moved from place to place. The houses were part of their chattel."

"Mobile homes, island style," Janet whispered to Stephen. "Fascinating." Tucked among blooming poinsettias, snow on the mountain trees and hibiscus, the cottages seemed so integral a part of the island that they, too, might have sprung up from the island soil. But they actually were portable, and rootless.

"No two of these homes are identical," John said, "but you will notice some common features. The wooden shutters at the windows are jalousies, and they can be battened down in the event of bad storms or hurricanes. On Barbados, we have a bad hurricane only about once a century. The last hurricane to hit this island with full force was Hurricane Janet in 1955."

Stephen gave Janet a sideways look and grinned. "Hurricane Janet—I can believe that."

As they approached the top of the island, the terrain became rocky and bare of vegetation. The first stop, the Animal-Flower Cave, was located on a craggy cliff near the most northerly tip of the island.

Janet and Stephen were scarcely halfway down the stairway into the cave when they realized they'd made a mistake not waiting until all the others had gone down before trying the descent. Stephen's stiff leg made progress painfully slow on the steep steps, and the line of tourists backed up behind them.

Janet took Stephen's arm and guided it across her shoulders. "Lean on me if you have to."

"We're going to fall and break both our bloody necks," Stephen whispered grimly, but with the wall of tourists pressing them from behind, he had no choice but to allow her to brace him as they continued their descent.

The wet rocky floors of the catacombic cavern were almost as treacherous as the stairs, but they finally found secure footing in an out-of-the-way area near a cave wall.

When everyone was in the cave, John pointed out the huge likenesses of a human hand and a turtle that had been carved into the stone roof and walls of the cavern by the seawater.

"As you explore the cave, look closely into the rock pools. You might be able to spot the sea anemones clinging to the stalagmites and stalactites," John told the group. "These sea worms give the cave its name, because some people think they resemble flowers as they open and close their tentacles."

The rest of the group struck out to explore the network of small rooms. "You can go with them, Janet," Stephen offered. "Just because I am an invalid—"

"Invalid, indeed," Janet replied. "Don't be melodramatic. I don't relish the thought of falling on my behind and landing on a wet stone floor any more than you do. Let's go watch the ocean."

He gave her an exasperated scowl that told her he knew she would be leading the pack of fellow tourists if she was not trying to be tactful about his inability to maneuver the wet floors with his stiff leg.

She smiled congenially. "It's all right, Stephen. Caves are not my thing. We've seen the hand and the turtle, and I can see a sea anemone anytime I like in the saltwater aquarium at the neighborhood pet store. I'd really like to explore the cliffs."

So they climbed the stairway unhurriedly. Stephen left his arm around her after they reached the cliff top, and Janet was glad. It seemed so natural being close to him after what they'd shared the night before, so natural smelling his cologne and feeling the mass of his body next to hers.

From the edge of the cliff, they watched the surf crashing into the rugged stones below. The waves were magnificent, colliding against the rocks with breathtaking force and then splintering into a wall of droplets that hung suspended in the air before collapsing back into the water, becoming once again part of the great salty vastness of the ocean.

Janet sucked in a lungful of brine air and released it slowly. "I've always wanted to see cliffs like this," she said. "It's like being in a gothic novel. You almost expect Rebecca de Winter's boat to come washing ashore with its telltale holes."

"Who is Rebecca de Winter?"

Janet was appalled. "Don't tell me you've never read *Rebecca*."

His blank expression told her exactly that.

"Then you've seen the movie?" she said hopefully. "Alfred Hitchcock made it, with Joan Fontaine, and Judith Anderson and Laurence Olivier and George Sanders."

Still a blank look.

"How could you not have seen or read *Rebecca*?"

Stephen shrugged his shoulders and gave her an it's one-of-life's-little-mysteries look. "What kind of story is it?"

"Oh, it's wonderful. It's about this unsophisticated young woman who falls in love with this divine, wealthy man named Maxim de Winter. He loves her because she's so innocent and unpretentious, you see, so they get married, and he takes her home to his mansion called Manderley, which is on a cliff like this, overlooking the sea."

"And they live happily ever after."

Janet gave him an exasperated scowl. "That's only the beginning of the real story. You see, his first wife, Rebecca, who was stunningly beautiful, had drowned, and the new wife becomes obsessed with her, because Rebecca was so beautiful and sophisticated and everyone had loved her so much. And the housekeeper, who had worshiped Rebecca, keeps all her things around, like silver hairbrushes with *R*s engraved in them, and she maintains Rebecca's room like a shrine. And she bullies the new wife unmercifully, and tells her Maxim could never love her the way he loved Rebecca."

"And they say good help is so hard to find."

"Please don't make fun of it. I'm not telling it very well, I guess. You have to read it, or *see* it, the way the tension builds while she keeps finding big, ornate *R*s on everything. Daphne Du Maurier deliberately didn't give the heroine a name; it was a subtle literary device to make the reader feel her lack of identity when she came up against the legend of Rebecca."

"What happens? Does she find out Rebecca is really alive?"

Janet shook her head. "Everything changes when a ship is wrecked on the rocks and a diver finds Rebecca's boat, with a body inside, and the authorities decide to raise it to find out whose body it is, because they'd already buried someone Maxim had identified as Rebecca. And Maxim tells the heroine that he killed Rebecca in an argument and then deliberately sank her boat with her body aboard, and identified a body that wasn't hers so no one would find out."

"That must make her feel very secure, knowing that she's married to a murderer."

"It does, in a way. You see, he *hated* Rebecca, because she was cold and self-centered and something of a nymphomaniac. And the heroine is relieved that he hated Rebecca, she's *glad*, because she'd been so convinced that he couldn't love *her* as long as he still loved Rebecca. That's what makes it so romantic—that what he did wasn't as important as that he hadn't loved Rebecca and, therefore, is free to love her."

"Does he get caught?"

"That's their fear, of course. When the authorities discover that the boat had been scuttled from the inside, they start investigating, and it looks like Maxim will be tried for her murder. Then they discover that Rebecca had found out she was terminally ill, with nothing but pain and a slow wasting away ahead of her. Maxim is acquitted because they assume she committed suicide."

She paused to catch her breath. "Of course, when he realizes that Rebecca deliberately provoked him into killing her, he still feels she defeated him, because she was able to manipulate him, even in death. And he's sad that his new wife has lost that look of innocence he loved about her, so they don't exactly live happily ever after, but they do find peace together after the crazy housekeeper burns Manderley to the ground."

She took a deep breath and, realizing how she'd gone on, glared at Stephen exasperatedly. "Why did you let me do that?"

"Do what?"

"Ramble on and on like that. I feel as though I've done one of those Classics of the World in Five Minutes."

"I loved hearing you tell the story. You were so passionate."

"You've got to see the movie. It won the Academy Award for best picture. It's on video. Promise me you'll find it when you get back to Canada."

"I'll watch on the giant screen in the lounge."

"But you have to read the book first. Promise me you'll read it."

"After such a review, how could I resist?"

She was pensive suddenly and stood there, as still as a statue, looking out at the restless ocean. "You'll go back to Canada and get busy and forget all about it."

Stephen crooked his forefinger under her chin and guided her face to his. "Do you have so little faith in my promises?"

She forced a laugh. "It was a silly thing to ask you to promise: watch an old movie and read a romantic novel, when obviously you don't like that kind of story."

"I want to see the movie, and when I do, I'll remember this cliff and being here with you." And with that, he kissed her.

Janet felt as though she'd been transported, at least momentarily, into the pages of a madly romantic novel.

It didn't matter that they were in Little Scotland on Barbados instead of England; that the cliff was not really a high one; that there was only a gentle breeze, and not a brisk wind to whip at their hair and clothes. None of those details mattered in the least. What mattered and marred the perfection of the moment, was the nagging reality that for them, happily ever after was destined to last only until his plane took off on Monday.

They'd been lovers for less than twenty-four hours and already the prospect of saying goodbye to him was tainting the perfection of the time left to them.

11

THE LANDSCAPE CHANGED again drastically as the bus headed south along the eastern side of the island. The conical Morgan Lewis Mill, the last of over five hundred Dutch-design mills that had once existed on the island, looked peculiarly at home surrounded by swaying palms and other tropical vegetation.

Soon after spying the mill, they approached their next stop, a scenic overlook atop Cherry Tree Hill, erroneously named for the mahogany trees that formed a canopy over the roadway at one point.

"You will notice the goats grazing on the hillsides," John said into the microphone. "These are not goats at all, they are Barbados sheep. They have very little wool because of the warm climate, and since they have so little hair, most visitors think they are goats. You can get a close-up view of these sheep when we stop. From this hill, you can also get the best scenic view of the island. Those of you with cameras should make sure they're loaded now."

Stephen had left his bulky camera at the hotel, but Janet had brought along her small point-and-shoot, and she dug it out of her shoulder bag. "My friends at work would be disappointed if I don't bring home pictures," she said.

"I'll take your picture at the top of the hill," Stephen said.

"Uh-uh," Janet countered. "I'll take *your* picture. You're my show-and-tell. Of course Ellie and Beth, my two best friends, are going to accuse me of paying you to let me take the photo."

Stephen laughed. "Why would they accuse you of something like that?"

"Because you're too good to be true. Single, gorgeous *and* nice. They'll never believe me. They're expecting me to come back with sunburn and sore feet, not . . ."

"Not?" he teased, amused by the blush creeping over her cheeks.

"Not . . . feeling the way I'm feeling this morning."

He gave her a reassuring hug. "I'm feeling the same way, Janet."

Remembering their experience on the cave stairs, they waited until the bus had cleared out before leaving their seats, and were the last to exit. The bulk of the crowd was already ascending the grade to the overlook, but a small cluster of passengers were gathered around a Bajan shepherd who'd been waiting for the bus with one of the scraggly-haired Barbados lambs, which he was letting the tourists pet and hold and photograph in exchange for tips.

"I'd really like to hold it," Janet told Stephen. "You don't mind waiting in line, do you?"

A few minutes later, Stephen observed Janet's face through the camera's viewfinder as the shepherd slipped the lamb into her arms. Her smile, so spontaneous and genuine, touched his heart. The lamb nudged its nose at her face and she laughed. Stephen snapped a photograph and wished he had brought his own camera.

"Be sure and get one with the shepherd," she said, motioning for the man to move within range of the camera. The old man moved slowly but did as she beckoned with a tired air of acceptance, as though he'd done it hundreds—perhaps thousands—of times before.

Stephen marveled at the contrasts in the tableau she'd assembled: the lamb, young, tiny and docile; Janet, fair skinned and lovely, her dark hair glistening in the sunlight; and the shepherd, ancient and gaunt, with sun-and-wind-leathered ebony skin, rheumy eyes and white-streaked hair. He took two photos in rapid succession and lowered the camera.

Janet turned to the shepherd to give him back the lamb, but he gestured for her to go on holding it, since there was no one else waiting. Stephen sensed her pleasure and noted the way she massaged the lamb's neck with infinite gentleness.

"Would you and your little friend like to see the best view in Barbados?" he asked, gesturing to the top of the hill.

The view awaiting them after the slow, trodding climb up the incline was worth the effort. From this high vantage point the trees, roads and houses in the valley beyond took on a storybook-illustration perfection. Trees and shrubs blended together into a backdrop of green, roads twisted like grosgrain ribbons dropped onto the earth, houses looked like painted matchboxes, and the entire scene was lighted by a brilliant sun suspended among cotton-ball clouds in a vivid blue sky.

"I had forgotten how beautiful mountains and valleys could be," Janet said, taking a deep draft of air and releasing it in a sigh. "Florida is so flat."

Her fingers stroked the lamb's neck. "I guess this barely seems like an anthill to you, compared to the Rockies."

"It's lovely, nevertheless," Stephen replied. "But not much good for skiing, I'm afraid."

"As much as I hate snow, I wouldn't suggest skiing without it," Janet agreed. "Those rocks would make for a bumpy ride."

She turned slightly toward him, so that the lamb was facing him. "Why don't you pet her?"

Stephen did so, rubbing the lamb between the ears with his forefinger. The lamb strained after his finger, nudging against it, and Janet said, "She likes you."

"You like her, don't you?" Stephen said.

"How could anyone not like something so small and guileless? Poor little scrubby-haired thing."

"Janet, would you excuse me? I'll meet you near the bus when it's time to board."

Concerned by his abrupt manner, Janet said, "Is something wrong?"

"There's something . . . I just want to check into something."

"I'll go with you," she offered.

"No, Janet. I . . . this is something I'd like to handle alone."

"But the grade on the hill, and your leg—"

"Janet, don't baby me. I am perfectly capable of walking down the hill unassisted."

"Oh," Janet said, feeling slightly rebuffed. "Well, if that's the way . . . I'll meet you at the bus."

She watched him start down the hill, limping slightly, and quelled the urge to dash to help him when his healthy foot landed on a loose rock and he had to save himself by shifting his full weight onto his injured leg.

Instead, she grinned at the inevitability of his saying the word she now recognized as his panacea for frustrating situations. Poor macho baby! What was it about men that made them insist on feeling invincible? Whatever it was, if he went skittering down the hill on his backside, she didn't want to see it. And he obviously didn't want her butting into his mysterious mission, so she directed her attention to the magnificent view of the valley and continued idly petting the warm little bundle nestled complacently in her arms.

She followed the general movement of the tour participants back to the bus some minutes later. Stephen was waiting for her as promised. "I see you made it," she said.

"Do I get a gold star for hill negotiation with a cane?"

Janet scowled at him a moment, then turned her attention to the lamb she was holding. "We'd better get this little girl back to poppa and get on the bus," she said.

"There's no hurry," Stephen said. "John is serving drinks, so it'll be awhile before we leave."

"Where *is* the shepherd, anyway?" Janet asked, noticing his conspicuous absence. Then, spying the old man's stoop-shouldered figure a good fifty yards down the road and walking steadily away from them, she sniffed exasperatedly. "I guess we're supposed to chase him down."

"You don't have to chase him down," Stephen said.

She gave him a sharp look. "If he—or you—thinks I'm going to just put this little baby down to wander around at will, then you're both wrong."

Stephen leaned forward and kissed her on her forehead. "You don't have to do that, either, Janet. The lamb is yours. It belongs to you. I bought it from the shepherd."

He laughed at the perplexed expression on her face as she absorbed the information.

"You *what*?"

"I bought it from the shepherd. It's a gift."

"Stephen!"

"You don't like it?"

"Of course I like it. I love it. It's tiny and cuddly and sweet. But what am I supposed to do with a lamb?"

"Enjoy it," he said. And then, smiling in the face of her skepticism, he added, "Only while you're here on the island. Just a few days. We'll have someone from the hotel bring it back to the shepherd after you leave."

"But that's crazy."

"What's so crazy about it? You like holding her, she likes being held. She even likes me. You said so."

"But—"

He rested his hand lightly on her shoulder. "I wanted to give you something *special*, Janet, something no man has ever given you."

"Well, you certainly succeeded! But what am I supposed to feed it? And where will I keep it. The hotel—"

"Janet, I have lived in a hotel all my life, and I can tell you that nothing is impossible with the proper arrangements. Won't you trust me to make them, as part of the gift?"

When she didn't reply, he coaxed, "So—do you keep the lamb, or do I have to hobble down the hill after the shepherd and give it back?"

Janet looked from the lamb, snuggled cozily in her arms, to Stephen, regarding her expectantly, so *hopefully*, and sighed softly. She spoke as though words were an effort. Her eyes were suspiciously overbright. "How could I not keep such a special gift?"

Stephen pulled her into his arms for a hug, lamb and all. She swallowed the sob that rose in her throat and buried her face in his shirt so he wouldn't see how close she was to crying. Silently accepting his strength, Janet choked back the bitter question that was foremost in her mind: *How am I supposed to say goodbye to you when I've fallen in love with you?*

They stayed there, hugging, until John called to them that the bus was about to leave. He treated the presence of the lamb on the bus with typical island nonchalance, announcing, "We seem to have acquired a new passenger," from the front of the bus as Janet and Stephen made their way to their seats, amid a chorus of, "Aw, isn't that sweet!" comments from the other passengers.

If the lamb was anxious about finding herself on a moving tour bus, she didn't reveal it. Lulled by the humming of the bus's engine and the warmth of the human body holding her, she curled up and fell sound asleep. Janet stroked her back absently. "Poor little thing. She looks like a Brillo pad."

She and Stephen looked at the lamb's scruffy coat, then each other, and smiled. "I think you just named her," Stephen said.

"I think you're right," Janet said, stroking the sleeping lamb's bony back.

They stopped for lunch at the Atlantic Hotel in Bathsheba. There, in that fishing village with rocky beaches, winding dirt roads and palm-trees-and-bungalows ambience, a little girl about six years old waited for the bus. She was barefoot, her head capped by irregular rows of pigtails that kicked away from her scalp at odd angles. She held a small bucket of shells she'd gathered and offered them for sale to the tourists.

With John's help, Stephen negotiated a deal for her to baby-sit the lamb while he and Janet ate lunch on the shaded terrace that overlooked Tent Bay, where the village fishermen launched their boats from the rocky beach each morning.

After a meal of chicken and peas and rice, Janet and Stephen hurried their dessert—moist and chewy coconut pie made from fresh, coarsely grated coconut—so they could get a head start on the long, twisting stairway that wound from the terrace down to the street.

They found the little girl near the bus, sitting on the shoulder of the road, bucket on one side, lamb tucked under the other arm. She scooped the lamb into her arms and scrambled to her feet as they approached.

"De lamb be fine, fine, fine. Lizzie do a good job," she said. She regarded them with soulful eyes as Stephen dug into his pocket for the Bajan coins he'd promised her. Only when she had them firmly in hand did she pass the lamb to Janet.

"Is your name Lizzie?" Janet asked, and the child nodded. "Her name is Brillo," Janet said, pointing to the lamb. "Can you say that?"

"Brillo," the child repeated with a shy smile. Then, sensing viable prey, she scooped up the handle of her bucket and held it out. "You see dese shells? Dey be pretty, pretty, pretty. I find dem dis mornin'."

"We don't . . ." Stephen began, but Janet checked him with a quelling look. The frown that passed fleetingly over his mouth metamorphosed into an indulgent smile. "Maybe we should take a look at those shells," he said. "I've got two little girls at home who might like some pretty shells from Barbados."

Lizzie shoved the bucket under his nose. "De be pretty, pretty, pretty."

"Why don't you show them to my executive purchasing consultant," Stephen said, grinning at Janet.

Lizzie gave him a blank look.

"He means me," Janet explained to the child. Passing Brillo to Stephen, she knelt and gestured for Lizzie to give her the pail. After carefully inspecting the entire inventory, she picked out half a dozen shells. "How much for all these?"

Lizzie had no problem understanding *that*. "T'ree dollars, Bajan."

"Sold," Janet said. She reached for her purse, but Stephen said, "Uh-uh. You're just the purchasing consultant, remember? I'll pay."

Juggling the lamb in one arm and her camera in the opposite hand, Janet snapped a photo while Stephen counted out the Bajan bills to the child. "You can caption that one, 'Canadian Tourist Taken in,'" he grumbled on the way to the bus.

"She was so darling, Stephen. Those big eyes and those funny little braids."

"You should at least have haggled a little, Janet. You could have gotten the whole pail for a dollar."

"But she was so cute."

"About as cute as Fast Eddy the con man. And you, Ms Granville—" he bent to kiss the tip of her nose "—were an easy mark. Buying seashells!"

"'Dey be pretty, pretty, pretty,'" Janet said lightly. Later, when they were settled in the bus, she said, "I take it these are for your nieces. Tell me about them."

Stephen considered the question a moment before replaying, "Nicole is twelve and giggles a lot, and Jennifer is ten and giggles even more."

"And Uncle Stephen is crazy about them."

He harrumphed at the notion. "It was just like Claire to have daughters instead of sons. I think my burden in life is to be surrounded by giggling females."

Janet bit back a smile at his expression of martyrdom. *You're not fooling me, Stephen Dumont.* She stroked Brillo's back. *Not one iota.*

Following a brief silence, she said, "Stephen?"

"Hmm?"

"I'm sorry about giggling last night, about... you know."

Stephen's mouth hardened into a petulant line.

"I wasn't laughing at *you*, Stephen. You're... well, an impressive man."

That earned her a grin. "Virile?"

She smiled back at him. "Yes. Virile."

Virile and bright and witty and considerate, and everything else I've always sought in a man, and I've gone and fallen in love with you.

Neither of them spoke again until the bus parked at St. John's Parish Church.

With Janet carrying Brillo, they meandered through the cliff-top churchyard, reading tombstones that dated back to the seventeenth century, then paused at the outside edge. Stephen stepped behind Janet, crossed his arms around her chest and propped his chin on her shoulder blade. They didn't waste words discussing the beauty of the rugged St. John's coast below; they simply enjoyed the sharing of it.

"Do you want to take a picture here?" Stephen asked.

"I don't need a picture." *I don't need an image on paper when I have the memory of this moment in my heart.*

"Nor do I," he said, and kissed her on top of the head before drawing his arms from around her so they could return to the bus.

12

"I CAN'T BELIEVE I'm doing this," Stephen said.

"Now you have something to write home about on one of your infamous postcards," Janet said.

"'Bathed a lamb today. Wish you were here.' Who'd believe it?"

"She's standing so still," Janet said, using her hand to funnel water onto the lamb's back. "You're being a good girl, aren't you, Brillo?"

They hadn't been sure how the lamb would react to water, but Janet had been adamant that if Brillo was going into the bungalow, even for short periods of time, she was going to have a bath first.

Far from panicking, Brillo seemed perfectly content to be lathered, scrubbed and rinsed at the faucet in the courtyard next to the pool. She stood docilely while Janet and Stephen rubbed and kneaded, glorying in the attention of the humans who had temporarily adopted her. With her skimpy coat wet, she looked more like a scrawny rat than ever.

"The cool water is probably refreshing," Stephen said. "I'm looking forward to leaping in the pool myself."

"Me, too," Janet agreed. "I think it's as hot now as it was at noon." Wrapping Brillo in the towel she'd brought for her, Janet lifted the lamb into her arms and cradled her like an infant as she roughed her sparse coat with the towel. Stopping abruptly, she looked at Stephen. "She's such a sweetheart, Stephen, such a special gift. I'll never forget your giving her to me."

Stephen was serious suddenly. "I wouldn't want you to forget me, Janet."

Her eyes told him what she felt even before she put it into words. "There's no chance of that."

A pregnant silence fell between them, unbroken until Brillo baaed unexpectedly. Petting her reassuringly, Janet said, "She'd probably like to move around a little."

Talking soothingly to the lamb, Stephen took the leash he'd fashioned from a clothesline bought at the Rockley store and slipped it around her neck. Then he tied the opposite end of the line to the pedestal of the patio table. Brillo walked around, testing the boundaries of the tether, then began nibbling enthusiastically on the dry oatmeal Janet poured into a plastic bowl.

"We don't have to worry about her starving," Stephen said.

"Obviously not," Janet said. "Ready for a swim?"

The sun was in its final stage of setting by the time they got out of the pool. Janet picked up her towel and, blotting her face, sank into a patio chair and sighed languidly.

"Tired?" Stephen asked.

"Uh-huh," Janet said. "Touring can be exhausting." She sighed again softly. "And I didn't get much sleep last night."

"Why's that?" Stephen asked, the sensual suggestion in his grin belying the attempted innocence of the question.

"You snore!" she said, parrying the cocky grin with a smile.

Stephen laughed. "As if we did enough sleeping for you to find out!"

"We'd get more sleep if we went to our separate bungalows tonight," she suggested.

Stephen dismissed what he obviously felt to be a ridiculous suggestion with a chortle of laughter. "The way you look in that swimsuit? The way you wiggled around in those shorts all day? Not a chance, lady."

"Are you saying you crave my body?"

"Every square inch of it." Taking her hand in his, he guided her to her feet. "Come on. We're wasting time." A muscle flexed in his jaw as a grave expression settled on his face. "Heaven knows we've precious little of it to waste."

A scant twenty minutes passed between the time he left Janet to go to his bungalow to dress and the time Janet answered his impatient knock at the door of her bungalow.

"I'm not dressed yet," she said, poking her face around the door she'd opened only inches.

"Good." Stephen determinedly pushed his way inside the bungalow, then lazily admired the rather skimpy sarong she'd fashioned from a hotel towel. "I'm glad I hurried."

She managed to utter only the first syllable of his name before he was kissing her and the towel was a puddle of white terry cloth on the floor.

Hours later, they called for a taxi and went to Shakey's Pizza for a midnight snack.

On their return to the Rockley, they made sure Brillo was securely tied to the patio railing of Stephen's bungalow and that her water dish was full before retiring to the air-conditioned haven of Stephen's bedroom where they made love, catnapped, made love again, then fell into a satisfying deep sleep that lasted almost until noon the next day.

They hiked to the Rockley grocery for picnic supplies, then made sandwiches on the patio of Stephen's bungalow. After finishing their own meal, they tore up bread and tossed it to the doves, sparrows and blackbirds who were never far away when food was around.

Brillo nudged Janet's knees with her nose, begging for more oats. Janet poured a scoop of oats into her palm and laid her hand on her thigh so Brillo could reach it. The lamb munched happily.

"She's certainly adapted easily to living with human beings," Stephen commented.

"Uh-huh," Janet sighed. The midday sun was high overhead, the grounds were green and lush, and she was sitting in the shade with her lover, feeding birds and lambs and feeling utterly replete. "I could stay here, just like this, forever," she said.

"Would you stay another week?" Stephen asked.

Janet turned to him, surprised, and he continued, "We could rent one of those little Jeeps and explore the island, and at night . . ."

Janet swallowed the lump that had formed in her throat. She didn't need Stephen telling her with his husky bedroom voice what they could do with another week of nights on the island; she knew only too well. They could fall even more deeply in love.

She was already counting the hours they had left, viewing time as a ruthless enemy, wondering how she would say goodbye to him when he left for the airport Monday morning. "I can't stay another week," she said flatly.

I can't fall that much more in love with you and then tell you goodbye.

"I need more time with you, Janet," Stephen said. "It's inconceivable that the day after tomorrow I'm supposed to hug you goodbye and get on an airplane and all this will be over. It's . . . all wrong."

Janet fumbled urgently for the right words to convince him that extending their stay would be a mistake. The right words—and the courage.

"My job," she said. Her voice cracked, so she cleared her throat and started over. "They're expecting me back at work Thursday. And my ticket is nontransferable and nonrefundable. I couldn't possibly afford another ticket, much less another week. I was pushing the limits of my budget when Trudy backed out and I ended up paying full price for the bungalow instead of halving it."

"If it's only a matter of money. . ."

She shook her head. "Please don't offer, Stephen."

Stephen's mouth compressed into a hard line as he clamped his teeth shut against the argument that he could easily afford an airline ticket for her and an additional week at the Rockley for the two of them. He wished he could make her understand that money didn't matter, that she was special to him, that he desperately wanted more time with her. But her meaning had been clear: she didn't want him to cheapen what they'd shared by putting her—at least in her own mind—into the category of bimbo-of-the-week.

Damn his sisters and that whole bimbo business!

After a long silence, he asked, "Is there anything special you wanted to do today?"

She shook her head. "No. You?"

"I need to shop for my family. The stores might not be open tomorrow, and there'll be no time on Monday before I leave."

"I'm always ready to shop," Janet said. Did the levity in her voice sound as false to him as it did to her own ears? Was he really getting on an airplane on Monday?

"Bridgetown again?" Stephen asked.

"There's an arts and crafts village near Bridgetown where the local artisans have their shops," Janet said. "It's on the list of places I wanted to go."

"Bus or taxi?" Stephen teased.

Pelican Village was a jumble of unpretentious stall-like shops. Stephen and Janet took a preliminary walk through the entire complex, getting a general overview of the Bajan batiks, handwoven baskets and place mats, wall hangings, aromatic *khus khus* root items, wood carvings, shell knickknacks, leather items and pottery offered for sale. Then, over iced drinks in the central snack stand, they discussed what Stephen would buy.

With Janet's guidance, he decided on batik for his mother and sisters, rag doll pajama holders for his nieces and mahogany wood carvings for his father and brother-in-law.

With the major decisions made, they set out to do the actual purchasing. Because of his merchandising background, Stephen was a conscientious and discriminating shopper. While most men would have grabbed a couple of the rag dolls and tossed them onto the counter, he carefully studied the facial expressions on at least a dozen of the dolls before picking the ones he thought matched the personalities and temperaments of his nieces.

In the wood carver's shop, he held the mahogany carvings in his hands, then lifted them into the light from the window, perusing them from all angles before picking out a bird for his father and a dog for Claude.

"Claude is crazy about dogs," he told Janet as the clerk bundled the carvings in tissue. "It is a family joke. Claire says he married her for the Dumont dogs."

"You raise dogs at the Chalet?"

"Only two. Saint Bernards."

Janet smiled delightedly. "Do they have brandy kegs around their necks?"

Stephen shook his head. "Ours are pets, not working dogs. But the guests love them. My father bought the first pair when he opened the Chalet, and we've kept a pair around ever since. We name them for Swiss cities, Mortie for Saint Moritz, and Bernie, for Bern."

"I'd love to see them!" Janet said, and realized too late the implications of the statement.

"Perhaps this summer..."

Perhaps I could visit you, and feel the same way all over again when I have to tell you goodbye? Janet thought. "It's difficult to get vacation time in the summer," she said. "The Magic Kingdom is packed."

"Because of school vacations. Of course," Stephen said, his disappointment obvious.

They reached the batik boutique. He was less comfortable in the sea of scarves, blouses, skirts, dresses and caftans than he had been among the wood carvings and dolls. After a long deliberation, he decided on caftans because of the one-size-fits-all advantage. Price, apparently, was not a particularly important consideration.

He chose bright colors, with a different motif for each woman, settling quickly on butterflies for Claire and birds for his mother. "And now Brigitte," he said, frowning at the plethora of remaining designs.

Turning to Janet, he cocked an eyebrow. "Any suggestions?"

"I take it she's not the flower type."

"No. Not Brigitte."

"The fish are attractive," Janet said, spreading the bottom edge of a caftan so they could see the predominantly turquoise-and-yellow design that depicted fish swimming in the sea.

"Yes. Fish will do nicely," Stephen said, then muttered, "one can only hope they're piranha."

Janet had to bite back a laugh at his dry sarcasm. "Still holding a grudge over the . . . er, Jungle Stalker episode?"

Stephen sniffed exasperatedly in response and draped the fish caftan over his arm with the others.

An exquisite cotton dress was displayed on the wall behind the counter. Pristinely white, it was elegant but simple, with a yoke of cutwork lace and long, flared sleeves that ended in gentle scallops. Delicate inserts transformed the ankle-length tapered skirt into a true flare, and the bottom edge of the dress, like the sleeves, was finished in gentle scallops.

While Stephen was signing the charge slip the salesclerk had written up, the clerk followed Janet's admiring gaze to the white dress. "Is pretty, no?" she asked, stretching out the adjective in the way peculiar to the island patois.

Janet nodded and the clerk said, "It is an original by one of our island designers. De cutwork and scalloped edges are hand finished."

"It's very elegant," Janet said, not even bothering to look at the price.

"Perfect for an island wedding, no?"

"Yes," Janet agreed. "It would be ideal for a wedding." She could easily imagine a barefoot bride wearing the white cotton dress on the beach.

Stephen could just as easily imagine Janet in the dress, feminine and innocently desirable. He started to suggest she try it on, but checked himself. He would have been happy to buy it for her, but he knew she wouldn't permit it. That disturbed him. If she had the dress, she would be forced to think of him every time she wore it back in Florida. He wanted her to think about him when she went home, to remember the time they'd spent together, the special affinity between their bodies and souls.

She interrupted his train of thought when she turned to him and said, "So, we're finished!"

He looked down at the bundle of plastic shopping bags he'd accumulated and gave her that familiar grin. "We'd better be. If I buy anything else I won't be able to get my suitcase closed."

The reference to his suitcase pained Janet. She was trying very hard not to think about his leaving, about spending her last night on Barbados without him, about wondering for the rest of her life what would have happened if he hadn't been born a Dumont, a man who, even by his name, was destined to be a part of the mountains—and if she hadn't almost frozen to death on that Minnesota roadside.

Since they had just agreed they were finished with their shopping, she was surprised when he ushered her into a jewelry store, seemingly on impulse, and told her he wanted to buy her something, a memento of the island. She was torn between the propriety of accepting an expensive gift and her own selfish desire to have something tangible that he'd given her.

It was Stephen's eyes that decided the matter. They settled on her face adoringly and pleaded with her silently. *I want you to remember me, Janet.*

As if I needed a reminder. As if I won't always remember a scrubby little lamb you bought me, and the way you hate sand in your pants and the way you combed the braids out of my hair with your fingertips.

Looking away from him so that he wouldn't see the tears welling in her eyes, she nodded her acquiescence while her heart shattered into a million tiny pieces.

After much debate, they selected a salmon-colored coral pendant set in gold, and Stephen insisted on buying her a slender gold chain so she could wear it immediately, although she assured him she had a gold chain at home. She held her hair off her neck while he put it on her. After closing the clasp, he dipped his head to kiss her nape.

Janet closed her eyes and, just for a few seconds, let her shoulders fall back against his chest, leaning on him because she needed his strength. Then she stiffened her spine and stepped away from him while he took care of paying for the necklace.

The knowledge of their imminent parting was a silent presence that accompanied them into the taxi. They were both uncommonly quiet until the cab approached the business district of Bridgetown and Stephen said, "We need to stop here. I'd like to go in the drugstore." Then with a warm, knowing grin, he leaned forward and whispered, "I, for one, am not consumed with a dying need to find out what a Banana Banger looks like."

Janet was holding the pendant in her fingertips, thinking that she'd like to give him something special to remember her by. There was only one thing suitable she could think of, and it was a long shot. Still, it was worth a try.

"I'm going to run into Cave Shepherd while you're in the drugstore," she told him.

"They're just a few blocks apart. Why don't we go both places together?"

"No, I—" She took a breath. "I want to check for something. And if they have it, I'll surprise you with it at the right time."

"Find what you were looking for?" he asked later when she met him at the designated street corner. He needn't have asked though, because she was grinning like the Cheshire cat and carrying a Cave Shepherd shopping bag.

"Uh-huh," she said.

"And that's all you're going to tell me."

"For now," she said smugly. "How about you? Did you get what you were after?"

He held up a small bag. "Mission accomplished."

Back at the Rockley, they cooled off in the pool, made love, then showered together before dressing for dinner. They went to a restaurant called Angry Annie's, chosen simply because they'd seen an advertisement and liked the name, and had wonderfully messy barbecued ribs with Bajan rice. And just when Janet was sure she couldn't down another bite, Stephen ordered ice cream for dessert, because he knew she loved it.

They took Brillo on a leisurely stroll around the golf course after returning to the hotel, and then went for a midnight swim. Their lovemaking afterward was thorough and bittersweet. Constantly aware that their time together was coming to an end, they made love as though they had an eternity in which to discover and pleasure each other. They reveled in the slowness, touching, kissing, loving unhurriedly as though mocking the clocks that ticked away, marking the passage of moments they would be unable either to retrieve or expand.

Then, exhausted, they fell asleep cuddled together, closing their eyes and their minds against the awareness that they would be waking up to their last day together.

And as though their minds and bodies were subconsciously rejecting reality, they slept very late on Sunday morning. Janet awakened to a pleasurable shower of fleeting kisses on her shoulders that became a torrent of lingering kisses elsewhere. Stephen traced over her breasts with his lips, teased her with his tongue and drew on her nipples as though he could take succor from them that would give him the strength to leave her. He kneaded her buttocks, filling his hand with her female flesh as though he might, if he wished it intensely enough, hold on to her forever.

Just as greedy for the feel and taste of him, the tactile memories, Janet slid her hands over his hard thigh muscles, running her fingers into the mat of hair that covered them as though seeking, in that tenuous threading, a way to anchor her body to his. She touched his testicles and then moved her hand higher to encase his swollen organ in her hand, glorying in the way it swelled and hardened even more at her touch. She bent and kissed him there, and he groaned with the intensity of sensation. Sitting up, he grasped her shoulders and guided her onto the mattress next to him.

An hour later, they were on the patio, using the last of their picnic supplies to make lunch. Brillo was there, begging for oats. The birds were back, too. The blackbirds watched them from the high limbs of the trees, the swallows from the shrubbery, and the doves walked in circles on the lawn, waiting for easy handouts.

I'll never forget this, Janet thought. *Not a single detail of it. For the rest of my life when I see a lamb or a blackbird or hear a dove cooing, I'll remember sitting on this patio with Stephen Dumont, wishing we could freeze this moment and keep living it for the rest of our lives.*

"I'll remember this every time I eat a ham sandwich for the rest of my life," Stephen said, startling her with the voicing of thoughts so close to her own. "Janet—"

She turned to him, touched his arm with her fingertips in anticipation, waiting for him to continue, wishing against all logic that he would tell her he was madly in love with her and beg her to come to Canada with him.

But he didn't. He raised his hand to caress her cheek. His lips poised to speak, then slid back into repose before compressing into a hard line of frustration; he shook his head slowly, sighed and tossed a handful of crumbs to the doves.

Ditto, Janet thought, her chest aching with frustration.

They spent their last day doing very little except enjoying each other's company. They took Brillo for a complete circuit of the Rockley grounds, frolicked in the pool and lounged poolside.

Janet created a phony excuse to return to her bungalow and made a phone call related to the mystery gift she'd purchased at Cave Shepherd. When she hung up the phone, she crossed her fingers and sucked in a deep breath, hoping intensely that everything would work out the way she had planned.

They had dinner at the Rockley that night. There was a tuk band, a fire-eating demonstration and the inevitable limbo contest. Janet excused herself, saying she was going to the little girl's room, and took care of the final details of her surprise.

The band was beginning to play "Yellow Bird" when she returned, and Stephen rose as she approached the table and gestured toward the dance floor. "I suppose you could say this is our song," he said as they began to dance.

"Ours and several million other couples'," she said.

"The song doesn't matter. This—" his arms tightened around her "—this is what matters."

They left soon and made love again with that profound slowness that defied the irrevocable passing of time. Afterward they lay together in silence for a very long time before Stephen lifted her hand, wove his fingers through hers and whispered her name.

"If you're going to say something sentimental, please don't," she said. "I'd just cry, and we'd exchange a lot of silly platitudes. We both know all the things we should be saying. Let's say them silently."

He nodded. His beard-roughened cheek brushed her temple as he moved. After a pause, he said, "Is there anything about Florida you don't like, Janet?"

"That's an odd question."

"It's a selfish question. When I think of you living in Florida without me, I want to know that your life isn't entirely perfect. So tell me what will keep your life from being perfect."

She didn't reply immediately. "There has to be something you don't like about Florida," he prompted.

"Promise you won't laugh?"

"At what?"

"At what bothers me about Florida."

"Why would I laugh, Janet?"

She exhaled heavily. "Okay. I'll tell you. It's the crawly things."

"Crawly things?"

"I knew you'd think it was silly."

"No, I don't. I just don't know what you mean by crawly things."

"Bugs," she said. "We have palmetto bugs that look like giant roaches and *fly*. And insects! I could kill a dozen bugs a day for a year, and never kill the same kind twice. I've had a running battle with mealy bugs on my houseplants ever since I moved there. I have to keep a soap solution in an atomizer to spray my plants."

She snuggled a little closer to him. "And lizards. There are millions of lizards. They're brown with black markings, and they look like miniature dinosaurs. You can't walk down a sidewalk without half a dozen of them scurrying in front of you and the shrubbery rustling because you've startled them. And I'm not even going to talk about the snakes and alligators."

She stopped abruptly. "Is that what you wanted to hear?"

"It was perfect. Now when I think of you, I'll think about you fighting with the mealy bugs and dodging lizards, and it won't hurt as bad as thinking your life is perfect."

There was a silence, and then he said, "But I wish you hadn't mentioned alligators, Janet. Now I'll worry about you getting eaten up by one."

"Not a chance," she assured him.

They were almost asleep when he said groggily, "You never showed me the mysterious surprise from Cave Shepherd."

"Maybe I'm planning on hiding it in your suitcase," she said, reasoning that since she'd used the word *maybe*, she hadn't told a fib at all.

13

"STEPHEN." Janet dropped a kiss onto his cheek. "Stephen. Wake up."

He opened one eye and groaned. "It can't be morning."

"It's not quite five."

Stephen sat up, rubbing his right eye with the back of his hand. "Four. It's *four* something?"

"I have a surprise for you," she said. "Get dressed."

"A surprise?" He shook his head to clear it. "At four in the morning?"

"We'll never make it if you don't hurry."

We're running out of time. Oh, Stephen, don't you realize our time is running out?

"Where are we going?" He'd dressed finally, and she was leading him out of the bungalow.

"I rented a Mini-Moke," she said.

"A what?"

"A Mini-Moke. One of those Australian all-terrain vehicles the tourists drive around in."

"Janet . . ."

"Shhh. You're going to wake up the whole courtyard."

He whispered, but it was an urgent whisper. "Where are we going in a Mini-Moke at four o'clock in the morning?"

"I've got directions, but you'll have to navigate. It'll be difficult enough to remember to shift gears and drive on the left without trying to read directions at the same time." She unlocked the doors and tossed her purse and tote bag into the back before settling into the driver's seat and starting the engine.

"Fasten your seat belt," she ordered, shortly before chugging the Mini-Moke out of the parking space.

"Gladly," he said as the vehicle lurched toward the main driveway in grasshopper glides. "You do know how to drive a standard, don't you?"

"Of course. They drew me a diagram of where the gears are when I signed for it. Besides, my father used to have a standard, and I drove it okay."

The gears screamed in protest as she shifted from second—into fourth. "It'll just take me a few miles to get used to shifting again."

"I can drive a stick," he suggested tactfully.

"With your sore leg? Anyway, I'm the only one authorized to drive the car because I'm the one who rented it, and I didn't have your driver's license number."

They compromised by letting Janet work the clutch on Stephen's command, while Stephen handled the stick. It worked well as she navigated her first right turn—particularly tricky to one unaccustomed to driving on the left side of the road. "There isn't much traffic," she said.

"I wonder why not," Stephen said. It took him perhaps fifteen minutes to realize they were following the same route the tour bus had traveled. He was consumed with curiosity, but he didn't ask where they were going. She wanted to surprise him—as if waking up at four o'clock wasn't surprise enough. He'd gone to sleep holding her in his arms, dreading the morning because he knew that even though they'd make love, it would be weighted with the awareness of his leaving. And now they were in a Mini-Moke, traveling up the left side of the highway toward only she knew where.

He studied her profile as she drove. Her features were tense, and not just with the driving. He'd been watching the tension build in her while their time together ticked away; he'd not only felt it in the intensity of their love-making, he'd *shared* it.

In the predawn darkness, the picturesque chattel houses looked artificial, like flat images painted on a stage backdrop. It suddenly seemed that everything about the island was slightly unreal. Except for Janet. Janet was delightfully real. When he touched her, she was warm; when he hugged her, she was all woman-soft flesh.

Tilting his head back against the seat, he closed his eyes and thought of going home, back to reality, to the natural order of things. It was January, so there would be snow; there was snow, so there would be skiers; there would be skiers, so the chalet would be bustling. Dumontique would be doing a brisk trade, and there would be wood fires and hot gleuwein.

He exhaled a weary sigh. He dreaded going home, dreaded all the hoopla of his welcome, dreaded having his family ask about his holiday and press for information about all the bikini-clad bimbos he'd seen. How was he supposed to tell them about Janet? How could he explain the special relationship they'd forged in so short a time?

I met a woman who hates snow and gave her a lamb that had no wool? It made no more sense than this perpetual summer.

Back in Canada there would be wood fires and hot gleuwein—and no Janet. And now he was sitting in a

Mini-Moke wondering if everything at home would seem unreal without her.

Janet turned off the highway at the entrance to the Animal-Flower Cave. It was closed, of course, but she parked near the gate, facing the ocean. The headlights of the Mini-Moke stabbed futilely at the blackness beyond the cliffs. She turned off the engine, then the lights, and engaged the parking brake. The crash and slosh of saltwater against the rocks below became a roar in the black silence.

"What now?" Stephen asked.

"We wait for the sun to come up." She turned her face to his. "You've never seen an ocean sunrise, have you?"

She could barely make out the movement as he shook his head.

"Good." And then, as though she felt a compelling need to make him understand, she said urgently, "I wanted to give you something unique, like you gave me Brillo and the pendant. I wanted to share something with you that you'd never shared with anyone else."

Needing to touch her, he touched her hair. "You have. A dozen times over. Everything we've shared has been unique."

Her throat convulsed. "I don't want to spoil this by crying."

Unsure what to say, afraid of saying the wrong thing, he said nothing.

Finally Janet suggested, "Let's get the top down so we can see better. It's supposed to be easy."

The diversion of figuring out how to collapse the folding roof dissipated some of the tension that had built up between them. They climbed back into the Mini-Moke, this time settling together on the wide back seat. Stephen sat slightly sideways, his legs stretched out in the space between the front and back seats. Janet curled up next to him, knees folded, her backside pressed against his thigh, her shoulders braced against his chest. She picked up her tote bag and dug into it, then pulled out the shopping bag from Cave Shepherd.

"Do I get to see the mystery purchase now?" Stephen asked.

Nodding, she gave him the bag.

He could make out the form of a book in the darkness.

"I'll get you the flashlight," Janet said, and leaned forward, searching for it in the front seat.

Her round bottom strained against the khaki fabric of her shorts as she stretched, and Stephen reached out to caress her right buttock through the cloth, knowing before he touched her what that female fullness would feel like against his fingers.

"Fresh!" she accused playfully, and the alluring mound of flesh slipped out of his grasp as she dropped back onto the seat. She gave him the flashlight.

He directed the beam onto the cover and read the title aloud, "*Rebecca.*"

"It was sheer luck, finding it, but it *is* a classic, and I remembered that Cave Shepherd had a large book department. We can read it together while we're waiting on the sun, if you'd like."

His arms tightened around her. "I'd love that."

"I've written something very sexy inside and signed it with the date. You'll go home and put it on your bookshelf and forget all about it, and someday when you meet someone special and get married, your wife'll find it and ask you who Janet was, and you'll say, 'She's just a woman I met on vacation once.'"

"I could not call you 'just a woman,' Janet."

He couldn't imagine finding anyone else he'd rather spend his life with.

"Oh, but this is years and years from now, after you meet the woman you've been looking for all your life."

You're the woman I've been waiting for, he thought fiercely. *Damn it, Janet, why did you have to get trapped in that godforsaken car in a blizzard? Why did something beyond our control have to condemn our chances for happiness?*

"She'll ask you if we were lovers," Janet said, "and you'll lie, very kindly, and say of course not, that you hardly knew me, and you'll realize you can't even remember what my face looked like. But you'll remember watching the sun come up over the ocean, and you'll smile, and she'll be dreadfully jealous."

"I think you could write stories as well as this Daphne Du Maurier."

"I couldn't even come close." She twisted until her breast pressed against his chest and her face was just inches below his. "Oh, Stephen, it's not fair to ask for promises, but please remember this, the way we feel when we're together. I don't expect you to remember my face, but please remember coming here to watch the sun come up."

He raised his fingertips to her face, and traced her features lightly. "Fifty years from now, if I were blind, I'd still be able to identify your face by running my fingers over it like this."

Then, cradling her cheek in his palm, he kissed her, imbuing the kiss with all the things they couldn't say to each other, with all the things he couldn't voice but was desperate to tell her. When he drew away, she sighed aloud and let her head drop against his breastbone.

A muted whimper warned him that she was crying, and soon her tears bled through his shirt. He hugged her urgently and pressed his cheek against her hair. The scent of it was as familiar to him now as the scent of cedar smoke from the fireplace.

Oh, Janet, what have I done? Why did I start it, when I knew...

We both knew, he thought fiercely. *We knew it couldn't go beyond this island. We both knew and agreed to take what we could for as long as we could.*

But it shouldn't hurt so much. Give me a sign, encourage me, and I'll talk you into coming to Canada with me.

Where she'd be miserable all winter?

I'd keep you warm, Janet.

She raised her head from his chest and, wiping her eyes with her fingertips, sniffed resolutely. "I'll read. You hold the light."

She picked up the book, found the first page of text and read aloud. "'Last night I dreamt I went to Manderley again.'"

Her voice and the beauty of the narrative merged with the lulling cadence of the ocean slapping against the shore, creating a soothing symphony of sound. The story was not as important as the mood it conveyed, a blend of anticipation, sadness and inevitability.

"'There was Manderley, our Manderley, secretive and silent as it had always been...'"

Stephen listened to the soothing music of her voice, loving the sound of it, just as he loved the warmth and weight of her body against his.

There will be wood fires and gleuwein—but no Janet.

"'The terrace sloped to the lawns, and the lawns stretched to the sea, and turning I could see the sheet of silver, placid under the moon, like a lake undisturbed by wind or storm.'"

She stopped abruptly. He felt her body tense at the same moment he sensed the change in the light. He followed her gaze to the east, where a strip of light outlined the horizon above the water like a slender brush stroke of luminescent paint.

The sun itself emerged with arrogant slowness, first a spot of light, then a crescent, a semicircle. The brightness it spilled into the twilight was shocking, thrilling; the halo of light radiating from it vacillated over the ocean and was reflected in the vast mirror of that wet, undulating surface.

Janet and Stephen literally held their breaths as the bottom tip of the sun cleared the horizon and hung there for seconds that seemed like hours, a perfect ball of dramatic fire, before ascending into the sky.

When Janet turned her face to Stephen's, all the wonder and miracle of the moment were reflected in her eyes as she whispered, "You'll remember?"

They kissed, and the kiss, too, held the same sense of wonder and miracle. When it ended, they sat absolutely still until the sun was well into the sky and the ocean was a sea of reflected fire.

The island was beginning to awaken as they drove back to the hotel. The traffic was still light, but thicker than it had been earlier. Outside of the utilitarian phrases needed to coordinate their joint effort at shifting gears, Janet and Stephen conversed very little. With the signs of a new day had come the unavoidable awareness that his plane would be taking off by the time the sun reached its highest point.

At the Rockley, Janet turned into the lot of her courtyard, rather than his. Stephen reached for the door handle after she'd parked, but she stayed him by putting her hand on his arm. "Not yet."

He turned his face to hers expectantly.

"This is so—" she sighed, and squeezed her eyes shut "—difficult. We have so little time. Oh, Stephen, let's spend it making love, not talking. If we talk, I'll cry, and that's not the way it should be. We've been too happy to corrupt it that way."

He nodded. *A sign, Janet. Any sign.*

"We'll go to my bungalow this time," she said. "I took the box of condoms Brigitte gave you from the bathroom and put them in my bag." She smiled at the surprise that registered on his face. "I couldn't bear spending the rest of my life wondering what a Banana Banger looks like."

A silence followed, charged with all the things they were leaving unsaid. Finally, in a near whisper, she said, "I don't want to have to tell you goodbye and watch you leave. I want to go to sleep in your arms. You can leave while I'm sleeping and tie Brillo outside my patio on your way to the lobby. Do you mind doing it that way?"

"I want to do what is easiest for you, Janet."

"You won't get much sleep, but it's a long flight back to Canada. Maybe you can sleep on the plane."

Stephen nodded, although he knew he wouldn't sleep on the plane. How long would it be before he would sleep without missing her next to him?

"Stephen."

His eyes locked with hers.

"I'm not sorry. I'll never be sorry we were lovers."

"Janet..." he began, but she shook her head and raised her fingertips to his lips.

"Let's go inside. And let's not say another word to each other. We won't say another word, and I promise not to cry."

He made love to her tenderly, more slowly than ever before, taking time to kiss her in unusual places that made her feel loved—behind the knees, on the underside of her breasts, on the small of her back. He teasingly nibbled her shoulder, her earlobes, the smooth globes of her buttocks, her fingertips. He probed her navel with his tongue, and the moist womanly depths of her with his fingers.

The sounds she made were not the words they'd forbidden themselves, but they were testament to the pleasure he gave her. She touched the now familiar textures and lines of his body in the ways she knew brought him pleasure, and when they decided it was time, through silent, mutual content, she opened the foil pouch and they learned together what a Banana Banger looked like.

They laughed together softly, until the time for laughter passed and their lips came together for a searing kiss. Stephen coaxed her thighs apart and slid his hand down the top of her right leg and under her knee. He urged it up, bending, then groaned sensually as he looked down at her, at the part of her that was open to him now.

He positioned himself above her with deliberate slowness, watching the anticipation on her face, then closed his eyes as he thrust inside her, impaling her with his need to possess her wholly. No matter how far apart they would be later, he would remember this moment, how Janet belonged completely to him.

It was not a time for denial or analysis. He was captivated by the feel and sight and smell of her, by the velvet smoothness of her skin, the firmness of her breasts straining against his chest, the smell of her hair when he burrowed his face into it, the salty taste of the tears she'd shed earlier that lingered on her cheeks. For this moment, he belonged to her just as completely.

He touched her the way she needed to be touched, and she arched against him, crying out at the sweet, terrifying intensity of what he was capable of making her feel. Seconds later he found the same overwhelming release and rasped her name as he collapsed over her.

For several minutes they lay that way, bodies entwined. They clung to each other as though letting go would have disastrous consequences—as if by letting go, they would lose each other forever as, in fact, they were about to.

They parted only long enough for him to dispose of the Banana Banger, and then they curled together under the covers on their sides, bodies spooning as Stephen wrapped his arms around her. "I know we're not supposed to talk," he whispered, "but there is something I must tell you."

Although she made no discernible movement, he felt the tension come into her body. "I said your name just now, when I came. I've never called a woman's name before. I wanted to tell you that."

Her cheek rubbed his arm as she nodded slowly. Seconds later she felt the dampness of her silent tears, but said nothing. He had spoken; she could cry. He drew her closer to him, hugged her tighter. *Say something, Janet; give me a sign.*

Minutes later, she was asleep.

Checking his watch, Stephen calculated how much time he had before he must leave to pack and catch the airport shuttle. He fought the instinctive urge to sleep after a nearly sleepless night and the exertion of their lovemaking both before and after they went to see the sunrise. The warmth of her body was seductive, her hair soft and fragrant against his cheek. It would be so easy to curl up into that warmth and relax, to go to sleep breathing in the fragrance he associated with her.

"I'm not sorry," she'd said. She'd given him her lack of regret as a present.

When he could delay no longer, he eased away from her, feeling as though he were leaving part of himself behind. He dressed as quietly as possible and, anxious to leave before he lost his nerve, reached for the doorknob. But he stopped halfway through the door to get one last glance at her.

Asleep, she looked vulnerable. Her shoulders were silky and smooth and made his fingers burn to touch her just one more time.

"I'm not sorry," she'd said.

He walked to the bed and stood there, just watching her sleep and listening to her breathe. *I'm sorry, Janet,* he thought fiercely. *Not for loving you, but for leaving you.*

Bending over, he allowed himself the indulgence of touching her hair one more time. To do anything more would be to run the risk of waking her.

14

STEPHEN REMEMBERED very little about the Barbados airport except for the heat and the nice lady who kept taking care of him. Now, on returning there, his first impression was that the terminal was surprisingly small to support so much international traffic.

After checking his bags and paying the island's departure tax, he browsed at the small newsstand, purchased a newspaper and settled into one of the inevitably uncomfortable waiting area seats, hoping the time would pass quickly until his flight was called.

Six days of total lack of contact with solid news should have made him curious about what was going on in the world, but after skimming the headlines, he folded the paper and tossed it into the empty chair next to him. He got up and wandered around the terminal, examining with detached disinterest the displays in the glass walls of the duty-free shops, glad he'd already done his shopping and wondering if he should take home a couple of pints of island rum to prove to his family he'd gotten into the tourist mind-set.

On his third pass of the perfume store, a particular name caught his eye. Written in gold script on an ornate bottle, it was the designer fragrance Janet said she'd never be able to afford. A masochistic impulse took him inside the shop, where he found a tester for the fragrance and misted it into the air.

He recognized it instantly, the same scent she wore in her hair, only more concentrated because it was quality perfume instead of a grooming aid.

The woman behind the counter asked if she could assist him in some way.

"How is this packaged?" he asked.

She put three cellophane-wrapped boxes on the counter. Small, medium, large. He reached for the large and then remembered that Janet had said something about perfume not having a long shelf life once it was opened, and picked up the medium box instead. "Can you mail this for me, to the United States?"

"T'ere is a fee for mailing, but we can do it, yes."

He gave her his credit card, then found the paper with Janet's address. The sight of Janet's handwriting, pretty and slightly frivolous, made his chest tighten. He slid the paper across the counter. "This is where I want it sent."

The clerk had already made an imprint on the credit slip, and she took a pad of forms from under the counter and copied the address into the appropriate blanks. "I'll need your name and address and some identification," she said.

He gave her his driver's license and tucked Janet's address back into his wallet.

"Do you wish to include a note?" the clerk asked.

"A note?"

"We have some enclosure notes." She reached under the counter and brought out a heavy vellum card.

Stephen picked up the pen and realized he had no idea what to write on that small rectangle of paper. His mind composed several possibilities and discarded them one by one.

Love, Stephen.

Remembering you, and the time we shared. Stephen.

Hope you enjoy the real thing. Stephen.

Think of me when you wear this. Stephen

I'll never forget the way your hair. . .

He dropped the pen on the counter and made use of his all-purpose expletive.

"No card," he growled at the disconcerted clerk, and shoved his credit card back into his wallet.

The seats in the waiting area were as uncomfortable as ever. He tried the paper again, and found it as uncompelling as earlier. Then, remembering the book he'd tucked into his camera bag, he dug it out.

"I've written something very sexy in it . . ."

Curious, he lifted the top cover to see what she'd written.

To the only man on the face of the earth who could keep me warm in a blizzard.

15

JANET AWOKE with an instant awareness that she was alone in the bed. Running her hand over the sheet where Stephen had lain next to her, she found it cool.

She felt the betrayal of the coolness, that undeniable proof of his absence, bitterly. Then, discovering a deep wrinkle in the bedding, she traced it with her forefinger, cherishing the feeble evidence that he had been there, glad that his body had left a physical manifestation to prove he had been real.

Her head ached from the pressure of tears that stubbornly refused to flow. She'd stayed on the verge of sobs when he was with her, and she'd kept them in check only with iron resolve. Why, now, when he was gone and she was alone, did she find it impossible to cry?

She put on her swimsuit and a pair of shorts and went to the patio to check on Brillo. The lamb was there, safely tethered to the leg of the table and munching contentedly at the grass within reach of her line. As the door opened, she stopped her munching and ran to Janet's feet, bleating for attention.

Janet sat down on a patio chair and lifted the lamb into her lap. Brillo stilled instantly as Janet hugged her. It was then, as Janet cradled the delectable warm weight in her arms, that the dam broke. Huge, copious tears slid silently over her cheeks and dripped onto Brillo's back, that pitiful, nearly hairless, bony little back. The lamb jumped when the first tear hit, then calmed again as Janet rocked back and forth from the waist.

Oh, Brillo, he's gone. And tomorrow I'll leave, and it's back to Cherry Tree Hill for you. It'll be as though we were never here. That was the cruelest pain of all, the idea that there would be nothing left of them on Barbados, nothing of *them* left anywhere at all, except in the memories they held in their hearts and minds. She would leave not knowing if she'd ever be able to come back and visit the places they'd been together. Or worse, wondering if she'd come back time after time, with some futile dream of recapturing the magic of the days they'd spent together, only to discover again and again that it was the fact of their togetherness and not the setting that had spun the magic, and that without Stephen the magic was irretrievable.

Oh, Stephen, I feel so empty. It's the emptiness.

She'd been so content before she'd met him, happy with her job, her friends and her active social life. She wasn't one of those women who'd felt that manic pressure to be half of a couple. But now there was this vast emptiness inside her, a compelling, unfamiliar, unsettling sensation of being incomplete.

Janet suddenly remembered what her mother had said at the hospital, when the doctor told them that her father had died. She recalled it so vividly, her mother sounding lost and confused, turning to her and asking, "What am I supposed to do now? Part of me is gone."

The stock answer from well-meaning friends and relatives had been, "You just have to take it one day at a time."

One day at a time. Yes, it made sense. Stephen was gone, and she'd drive herself crazy if she thought about carrying this emptiness inside her for the rest of her life.

Stiffening her spine, she sucked in a fortifying breath, held it, let it out slowly. She would think about today, focus on getting through the next hour. It was her last day on the island. Tonight there would be the packing, but today she was free to do whatever she wanted. She even had the Mini-Moke, although she wasn't crazy about the idea of driving in the heavy daytime traffic without a navigator.

In the end, she decided to stick with her original plan of going back to the beach. She'd saved the beads Stephen had taken out of her hair with the intention of getting her hair braided again so she could go home looking like a tourist. He'd put them into the plastic bag that had once held the tacky postcards he'd bought for his sisters in Bridgetown. As she took the bag from the drawer and dropped it into her beach tote, the pain of remembering that afternoon in Bridgetown and the bus ride back to the Rockley was like a knife in her heart.

Oh, God, she thought, choking back a sob, will it always hurt so much? Surely, with the passage of time, there would be some numbing, some lessening in the acuity of the memories, some defensive mental insulation from the pain.

Just as she was getting ready to untie Brillo's lead, the telephone rang. It seemed to her as though her heart ceased beating in the eternity it took her to cross the room and pick up the receiver and utter a breathless hello.

"Janet?"

The connection was scratchy, but the voice was unmistakable. She tasted the bile of disappointment. "Mother. Hello."

"This is an international call, so I'll talk fast. I just wanted to let you know that your Aunt Sally and I won't be coming to the airport tomorrow with Uncle Dave. We won the canasta tournament here in the village, so we're going into the citywides."

"That's great news, Mother."

Motherly guilt oozed through the crackling line. "It's not that we're not anxious to hear all about your trip. . . ."

"It's all right, Mother."

"It's just that if we missed the preliminaries, we wouldn't stand a chance of making the finals."

"Uncle Dave and I will do just fine," Janet assured her.

"You don't mind?"

"Don't be silly. You won the local title. You can't let the village down."

"Well, if you're sure . . ."

Janet's hand lingered on the receiver when she put it back into place, as though by touching it she could will the phone to ring again. She'd been so sure it was Stephen calling from the airport. How long would every ring of the telephone bring a surge of futile hope into her chest that it might be his voice who spoke back from the other end of the line?

She drove the Mini-Moke to the central parking lot and turned in the keys, then, holding Brillo on her lap, waited for the beach shuttle. Perversely, on this day of all days, her fellow passengers were all honeymooners. One of the brides asked to pet the lamb and wanted to know where and how Janet had acquired her.

Janet choked on the word *friend* while answering the innocuous question, and had to clear her throat and swallow to moisten her mouth before going on. "Excuse me," she said.

Excuse me for choking while calling Stephen a friend. Friend was accurate, but inadequate. How inadequate! He'd been so much more than that. He'd been her lover. He'd been a part of her.

And now he was relegated to a brief mention. "A *friend* of mine on the tour saw how much I enjoyed holding her, so he bought her from the shepherd and gave her to me, sort of as a practical joke."

No, no! Not a practical joke. It was neither practical, nor a joke. It was impractical and wildly romantic, just the way he'd meant it to be. He was a cynic, but he knew I was a romantic, and he wanted to please me. Oh, Stephen, why did you have to be so wonderful? Why did you have to make me fall in love with you?

The ride to the beach was emotionally tortuous. The brides were so happy, so in love with their new husbands, so filled with optimism about the future that Janet found herself resenting them in a most uncharitable, ungenerous way. But she was only human, and she was hurting; Stephen was gone, lost to her forever, and the brides were there with their new husbands, touching and exchanging those smug lovers' smiles that closed out the rest of the world.

Janet was alone, and she felt keenly the isolation of being locked away from that special little world of lovers. In her heart she still was half of a couple, but in reality, the other half was gone. The only future she could see was a dark void of loneliness.

Time. She needed time.

How long would it take before she could see past that dark void and find light? How long before the memories became blurred and comforting instead of vivid and hurtful? How long before she could look back on the beauty of their time together and smile? Before she stopped comparing men to Stephen, using him as a yardstick of perfection no man could hope to live up to?

Relieved to be out of the van and away from the honeymooners and their newlywed bliss, Janet stopped at the beachside bar to fill Brillo's dish with clean water, and then carried it and the lamb to the beach. She tied the sheep's lead to the trunk of a palm tree, then rented a beach chair and stretched out to let the sun—the same sun she and Stephen had waited for on the north cliffs of Barbados—annoint her with soothing warmth. After a few minutes of that indulgence, she lathered herself with sunscreen and moved into the slender ribbon of shade cast by the palm tree.

Brillo poked her nose under the arm of the chair, nudging Janet's hip with her nose. Janet looked at the pitiful little critter with no hair and, despite her morose mood, laughed softly at the lamb's cunning and scratched her behind the ears. Appeased, Brillo baaed a thank-you, then settled down next to the chair for a nap.

Janet picked up the book that had gone ignored in her beach tote since her second day on the island and tried to get involved in the story again. It was a futile effort. She couldn't concentrate on one book when she kept remembering reading another aloud while Stephen held the flashlight on the page in the predawn darkness and the ocean crashed against the rocks.

She had abandoned the book in favor of people-watching when she spied Alice and, waving, gestured her over to the chair.

"Hi!" she greeted, when Alice was within earshot. "I was hoping to see you today. Do you remember me? You braided my hair last week."

Alice nodded. "I does r'member. You don't like de braids? Dey all combed out."

"I like them very much, but . . ." Another memory. It hurt to think of Stephen running his fingers through her hair, knowing she'd never feel him touch her again. It hurt to think about him laughing at her and assuring her she didn't look like a poodle when she really did. And then going into the bathroom to see herself in the mirror and finding him there wearing Jungle Stalker!

"I took them out," she told Alice. "I was hoping to find you here today. I'm going home tomorrow, and I was hoping you could braid my hair again."

"I happy, happy to braid it."

"I saved the beads," Janet said, digging into her tote for the small shopping bag and her comb.

Alice worked quickly and efficiently. When she'd finished, she took the hand mirror from her bag and gave it to Janet, who inspected the braids, tilting her head from side to side as she looked into the small mirror.

"Dey be pretty," Alice said, stretching the word for emphasis. "You friends be saying you look real Bajan."

"Yes," Janet agreed, forcing a smile. "That's exactly what they'll say. You do good work, Alice." She gave her back the mirror and paid her the agreed fee. Alice thanked her, pocketed the Bajan bills and walked up the beach in search of new customers.

Janet picked up the book again. Still unable to get interested in it, she snapped it shut and jammed it into her tote bag, then stood and peeled off her shorts. Brillo jumped up, frisky after her long nap. "Well, hello, sleepyhead," Janet said, reaching down to pat her. "You like my hair? What do you think? Am I a ten?"

Brillo answered with a wide-eyed stare.

"I'm going for a swim," Janet continued. "You can stay here and be a watch lamb, maybe chase a few butterflies."

The lamb continued staring at Janet with those baleful eyes, then followed her as she walked toward the beach. Reaching the end of her tether, she baaed pitifully.

Janet turned and planted her hands on her waist. "You wouldn't like the waves."

The lamb baaed again.

"Oh, all right." Janet knelt to untie her. "But only because you caught me at a vulnerable moment. I'm a little lonely myself today."

Cradling the lamb in her arms, she crossed the narrow sand beach and waded out into the water. The sound of the surf made Brillo nervous at first, but she grew accustomed to it quickly and relaxed, content in Janet's arms.

The sun, high overhead, was hot on Janet's face and shoulders. It contrasted nicely with the cool water that slapped over her thighs as she walked parallel to the shore. The beads on her braids clicked together as she moved, reminding her of the evening at the museum.

Stephen's plane would have taken off by now. He was probably halfway to Miami, on the first leg of his journey back to the winterland he loved, to the large, close family of giggling sisters and nieces who spoiled him rotten.

What would he tell them about her? she wondered.

"May I pet your puppy?"

Shocked from her thoughts, Janet looked down at the little girl who'd posed the question. She was about seven, blond, curly haired and slightly chubby.

"You can pet it, but it's not a puppy, sweetheart. It's a lamb."

The girl patted Brillo's head quite gently, as though she were accustomed to handling animals. "A lamb?"

"A baby sheep."

The child considered the possibility, then said matter-of-factly, "Sheep are fuzzy, with curly hair and black faces." Her accent was heavily British and quite charming.

"Not all sheep," Janet said. "This is a Barbados sheep. If she had lots of hair she'd be too warm."

"Does she have a name?"

"Brillo."

The little girl laughed. "That's a funny name."

Yes, Janet thought. A funny name for an absurd little pet. An insane gift from a madman—the most wonderful, most romantic madman on the face of the earth.

"Might I hold her?"

"If she doesn't mind your wet swimsuit," Janet said. "Here, we'll give it a try."

Apparently the lamb's early experiences with a progression of tourists made her oblivious to details as minor as wet swimsuits, for she settled docilely in the child's arms. "Oh, she's sweet," the child said.

"Yes," Janet agreed absently.

"Where did you get her?"

"She was a gift," Janet said.

"From your mommy?"

"No," Janet said dryly. "Not from my mommy."

The call from her mother had unsettled Janet. Not that she was miffed that her mother wouldn't be at the airport. It just drove home a truth that she'd been slow in realizing: her mother didn't need her anymore, at least not as a roommate. She'd come to grips with her widowhood and stayed busy. And unless Janet was mistaken, the widower from the village who had taken to dropping by for after-dinner coffee was interested in more than the apple pie her mother served with the coffee. Soon she would be in her mother's way.

Staring, unseeing, into space, she sighed. It was time for a change, time to break the apron strings, maybe move into an apartment of her own. She was up for a pay raise in March. Maybe if she was careful, she could buy herself a small condo.

Maybe you could move to Canada.

Her chest ached. *He only invited you to visit his Saint Bernards.*

It was a beginning. Maybe if the dogs loved her, he'd ask her to stay. It had worked for his brother-in-law, Claude.

"From who then?"

Janet blinked her attention back to planet earth and looked at the little girl holding the lamb.

"Who gave her to you?" the child persisted.

"A—" Janet was going to say the word *friend* again, but her breath caught in her throat when a glance at the shore showed her what she knew could not be real. Stephen could not be standing there. She was hallucinating because she wanted so desperately to see him.

She closed her eyes, took a deep breath and opened them again. He was still there, scanning the swimming area with a searching gaze. Then, spying her, he smiled broadly and started waving frantically.

She allowed herself a glimmer of hope.

"Amy!" The stern admonition came from a woman several yards away, causing the little girl holding Brillo to jerk around quickly.

"Come along now. You mustn't pester."

The child pressed the lamb into Janet's midsection. "I've got to go. Mommy's calling. Thank you for letting me hold your lamb."

Preoccupied with the figure on the shore, Janet took the lamb with only a mumbled acknowledgment of the child's polite thank-you. Stephen—it must be him, because if she was going to conjure up an image of him, her mind would put him in shorts and the short-sleeved shirts he'd worn on the island and not in heavy cotton jeans and a long-sleeved shirt. He was sitting down now and taking off his shoes.

Janet stood frozen, staring as he peeled off his socks and then fought to roll the tapered bottom of his pants into cuffs. Gingerly favoring his mending leg, he rose to his feet again.

His gaze locked with hers as he walked toward the water. She couldn't help but smile when he grimaced involuntarily at the feel of the sand under his feet, then set his jaw with determination as he continued across the narrow beach and into the water.

She took a tentative step toward him, but he was taller and in shallower water and made three steps to her one, arrogantly ignoring the resistance of the water that swirled round his ankles, then his calves.

All morning she had wished for the chance to see him one more time, touch him one more time, tell him she wanted nothing more than a future with him. And now, when he moved close enough to hear her, all she seemed capable of saying was, "Your pants are getting wet."

He smiled the smile that was uniquely his and looked at her the way only he had ever looked at her, adoringly, seeing her as no man had ever seen her before. "Always mothering me," he said. "Janet, are you going to nag me for the rest of my life?"

"Oh," she said as her feeling of control eroded away and was replaced by a flood of relief mingled with joy. She felt the wetness of tears spilling over her cheeks and didn't care about them at all. "Oh, I hope so."

He took her into his arms, nearly crushing Brillo in his impatience to feel her body against his, then reluctantly loosened his embrace when the lamb baaed in protest. Still staring at Janet's face, he lowered his head, and his mouth fused over hers for a probing, possessive kiss.

He dragged his lips off hers and said breathlessly, "I couldn't leave you. It felt all wrong. And then I read your message. Janet, there has to be a way we can stay together."

"There is," she said.

The certainty in her voice drew his undivided attention. Oblivious to the sound of the ocean, the wind and the tourists frolicking in the surf, he waited for her to go on.

She exhaled a sigh of something like impatience. "All you have to do is tell me that you love me."

"Oh, Janet." His chest ached with the strain of holding back. He cradled her cheek with his palm and pulled her head to his chest. "How could you not know that I love you?"

"I knew," she said. "At least, I hoped."

He slid his hands to her shoulders and then down her arms, and she raised her head from his chest to look at his face. "Marry me, Janet. I've checked all the details. We've already established the residency requirement. If we apply for a license today, we can be married at the end of the week."

"I'm supposed to leave tomorrow morning," she said, shell-shocked.

"I was supposed to leave *this* morning."

A strong wave crashed into them, drenching them to the waist, and they had to fight for balance. Brillo baaed again in protest.

"Let's go where we can talk," Stephen said, draping his arm across her shoulders possessively while they waded out of the water.

They tied Brillo to the palm tree and knew a moment's awkwardness when they suddenly found themselves face-to-face on solid ground.

"You're all wet," Janet said.

Stephen looked down at his drenched clothing, then at his feet, and frowned. "My feet are coated with sand."

A silence followed. Finally Stephen took her hands in his and guided them around his waist. Then he slipped his arms around her and pulled her close. He kissed her very gently. "Marry me."

She didn't reply and he kissed her again, lingeringly and not quite so gently. "I love you, Janet. Marry me. This Thursday."

"I..." she said, and hesitated. He pulled her even closer, kissed her until her knees went weak.

"If you don't say yes soon, we're going to create a public spectacle." The warning came out rather garbled because he hadn't fully broken the kiss, which he resumed with great skill and enthusiasm.

It was Janet who finally ended it by forcibly pulling away from him. "Yes!" she said breathlessly. "Yes, you madman, before you get us arrested."

16

"I HAVE SAND in my underwear," Stephen said. "I don't understand how it got there. My feet, I understand, but . . ."

They were standing near the seaside bar, waiting for the Rockley beach shuttle. "The van should be here any minute," Janet said. "You can take a shower as soon as we get back to the hotel."

"You have no idea the kind of morning I had. Have you ever tried to uncheck baggage already loaded on an international flight?"

"That thrill has eluded me, somehow."

"It's almost as bad as having sand in your underwear," he informed her. "And then there was the hotel. No rooms, they said. They wouldn't let me check in, and wouldn't take my word for it that you would let me share your bungalow. If Regina hadn't intervened, they wouldn't even have let me leave my bags behind the desk, or let me on the beach shuttle."

"Poor baby."

"I am not a baby, Janet. Do not 'poor baby' me. You braided your hair again."

"Yes."

Stephen forgot the sand in his pants long enough to give her a sensuous smile. "I guess I'll just have to take them out again." The smile faded. "But not this afternoon, unfortunately. We're going to have to hustle to make it to the Marine House and the post office."

"The Marine House and the post office?"

"Yes. We get the license at the Marine House. It's in Christ Church, so it can't be too far."

"And the post office?"

"A special stamp. In Barbados, getting married is like mailing a letter. You go to the post office and buy a stamp."

Janet sighed wearily. "Are you sure we're doing the right thing, rushing into this?"

"Do I have to convince you again?" The expression in his eyes turned positively lecherous, as though he rather hoped he might.

"I wouldn't put you through that when you've got sand in your pants," Janet said. "Although, heaven knows, it might serve you right for sweeping me off my feet and muddling up my judgment with . . . carnal persuasion."

Stephen suddenly grew very serious. "You don't really mind, do you? It's just that...we've been so happy here, and....I want it to be a private thing between us." He heaved a sigh. "If we wait, it'll just get more and more complicated. My sisters would want to turn it into the social event of the decade. As it is, we'll probably be the main attraction at the first Family Night that we're home."

"My mother—"

"Will she be hurt that you eloped? We could fly her here."

"She hates flying." She smiled. "Besides, she and my aunt are in a citywide canasta tournament this week. No, she'll be a little disappointed, but we'll have pictures, and...oh, Stephen, she's absolutely going to adore *you*. She'll be commuting back and forth to Banff regularly."

He was silent again, pensive. "Winters in Banff are not quite the same as in Minnesota. You shouldn't feel closed in at the chalet with so many people around, and it's not as though you'll ever have to get out in it if you don't want to, and . . ."

"And you'll be there to keep me warm."

"Always," he said, and kissed her.

She smiled wistfully. "I was so miserable when I woke up and you were gone. I'd go to the North Pole and make toys with you if you asked me to." Her eyes, slightly teary from the intensity of her emotion, locked with his. "I love you so much."

He cradled her cheek in his palm, and his eyes were warm on her face. "I love you, too, Janet. I want you to be happy."

A silence followed. Then she stiffened suddenly. "I just thought of something. Stephen, even if we stop in Florida for my things, I don't have anything to wear in Canada in January. I gave away all my cold-weather gear."

"I'll loan you my socks."

"I'm serious, Stephen. This is a real problem."

"You're going to be expensive, aren't you?" he said, grinning.

"I can't wear shorts and sundresses in Canada in January."

"You've got jeans, haven't you?"

She nodded.

"We'll pick up a couple of Icelandic wool sweaters here, and with a couple of Dumontique sweatshirts, a down jacket and a good pair of boots, you'll be all set. You can always borrow from Claire or Brigitte. They love rescuing people almost as much as you do. Chalet Dumont is very casual anyway. We mostly run around in sweaters and pants when we're not dressed for skiing."

"This from a man who was wearing cashmere at the Barbados airport!"

"I'm very glad that I was, too. If I had not been about to pass out from the heat, you would never have rescued me."

"You were about to pass out from Scotch whiskey."

"Does it matter? The important thing is that you rescued me. It scares me to death to think what would have happened if you hadn't."

"Poor baby. You'd have spent the entire week riding in taxis and trying to find a dozen bimbos."

He threaded his fingers through hers and gave her hand a gentle squeeze. "I need you, you know."

"Desperately," she agreed.

THEY WERE MARRIED the following Friday at dawn while standing on the north shore cliffs.

The video photographer they hired captured all the details and images for their families: Stephen in a black tuxedo and Janet in the white cotton dress she'd admired at Pelican Village, holding hands and repeating traditional vows before the minister dressed in maroon ceremonial vestments; the sun rising to glorious brightness over the blue-gray sea; the hauntingly beautiful melody of "Drink to Me Only with Thine Eyes" played by a solo flutist; and one tiny stubble-haired lamb curiously eyeing the pageantry from his tether at the top of the cliff.

They took Brillo back to Cherry Tree Hill before going to their hotel. Janet gave the lamb one last hug before putting her down in the grass in sight of the shepherd and his flock. Brillo hesitated, then began happily munching on the grass.

If there were tears in Janet's eyes as she whispered, "Goodbye, Brillo," they were destined to be short-lived. Now the joy in the memory of Stephen's wild, romantic gesture of buying the lamb for her would be sweet instead of bittersweet, because she had Stephen to share it with. He was there beside her, touching her, giving her the strength to let go of the past and move into the future. Their future.

Somehow, at the height of the tourist season, Stephen had managed to arrange a bridal suite overlooking the sea. She would have been content in the bungalow at the Rockley, but he'd insisted that they move, as a symbolic gesture of the significant change in their relationship. They had become lovers at the Rockley; in the honeymoon suite, they would know each other for the first time as man and wife.

He was quite a romantic at heart, this wild Canadian hunk she'd married.

It was more beautiful and moving than she could have imagined, having him undress her and love her with the sea churning just outside the double doors of the suite. He began by kissing the gold band he'd put on the third finger of her left hand, and then the top of her hand, and then her fingertips, whispering sweet, sentimental things between kisses. He told her how pretty she was, how desirable she was, how much he loved her because she cared about people, how much he needed her to care about him.

After their marriage vows were formally consummated, they lay together in the bed, listening to the ocean and each other's hearts. And then they talked, and he told her how easily she would fit into his family and life at the Chalet Dumont.

Their naked bodies were pressed together, their limbs entwined. Stephen lifted her hand to his lips, kissed it, drew in a deep, steeling breath and said, "I want you to be happy, Janet. Your happiness means as much to me as my own."

"I couldn't be happier," she said softly.

"I don't mean just this moment, or just this month, or this year."

A silence followed, warm and mellow. Then he continued, "I want you to make a promise to me, Janet."

He felt her cheek move against his chest as she looked up at his face expectantly.

"Promise me that if you're ever unhappy, you'll tell me, so we can do something about it."

When she didn't say anything, he continued. "I love my family, my country and my life-style. And I thought long and hard before I was able to ask you to give up those things in your life."

His arms tightened around her, as though by physically binding her to him he could bind her in all the other ways that counted, too. "I would not have asked you to give them up if I hadn't believed you could be happy with me."

"You didn't force me to do anything," she said. "Not even with your sensual blackmail. I'd rather be in Canada with you than in Florida without you. A person needs all kinds of warmth, and I can't get everything I need from sunshine anymore."

"I love you, Janet. If Canada doesn't work, if you are unhappy, then I'd rather give it up to be with you than to lose you. That's why I want you to promise you'll tell me if there's a problem, so we can solve it instead of letting it tear us apart."

"You would leave the Chalet Dumont and your family for me?"

"For *us*, yes, I would leave. If it was the only way to keep us together."

She burrowed her cheek against his chest and sighed contentedly. "I love you, Stephen Dumont."

"And you would tell me?"

"Yes. I would tell you."

A long silence ensued, but it was a comfortable silence, filled with their happiness and their contentment at being together.

It was Stephen who finally spoke. "What are you thinking, Janet?"

"About us. About the future. About how in the past two weeks I've rescued a drunk hunk, fallen in love, taken a lover, been given a lamb, been proposed to, planned a wedding, shopped until I've almost dropped, quit my job and gotten married. And how in a couple of days, we're flying to Florida, where we'll undoubtedly be surprised with a party, and I'll pack up everything that fits in the trunk of my car before we drive to Canada. Canada, Stephen! My God. And then there'll be your family to face and Family Night—are you sure you want to surprise them with an announcement at Family Night, instead of calling to prepare them?"

"Quite sure. It's a perfect plan. You'll leave me at the airport and drive to the chalet and check in under your own name." He grinned. "Your maiden name, that is. And the cake will be ordered, as well. Then, on Family Night, I'll take the mike and introduce you, and take great pleasure in watching Claire and Brigitte's mouths drop open when the waiters wheel in the three-tiered cake."

"But your father and mother . . ."

"They're Dumonts. They'll love it. And they'll love you, every last one of them. You'll be a member of the clan by the time they've heard the story of how you rescued me at the airport."

They fell silent again, both lost in thoughts of the future. Stephen thought about Family Night at the chalet and how she'd fit in, and a rather unpalatable thought crossed his mind. "I've never asked you, Janet," he said. "You don't sing, do you?"

"Sing?"

"Yes. You know. Sing. Or play a musical instrument. You don't play the drums or the trombone or anything *unusual*, do you?"

"No." A note of panic crept into her voice. "I don't need musical talent to be a Dumont, do I?"

He chuckled. "If you did, you'd be the only Dumont outside of my mother who had any."

"Good," she said, greatly relieved. "Because I have no talent at all for singing, and I don't play any musical instruments."

Stephen breathed a little easier.

"That's why I keep a box of kazoos."

"Kazoos?" he asked, feeling a prickle of apprehension crawl up his spine.

"Kazoos. You know, you hum into them and they make a crazy vibrating noise. It's a lot of fun when you get a bunch of people playing them at a party, because it doesn't matter whether anyone can carry a tune or not."

A vision came to Stephen of a third microphone set up for Family Night, of Janet standing there between his sisters with a brass-plated kazoo, of his nieces going through the dining room passing out kazoos. And he heard the dining room filling with the din of a hundred kazoos being played in unison.

An involuntary smile slid over his face. "I love you, Janet," he said, and rolled over to kiss his new wife.

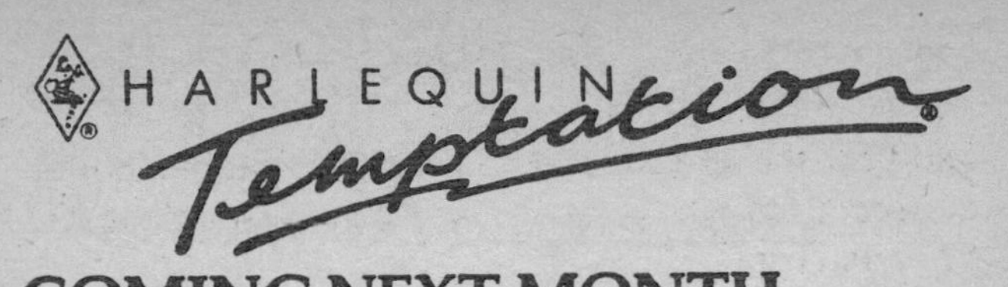

COMING NEXT MONTH

#301 SATISFACTION GUARANTEED Judith McWilliams

Kiley Sheridan, a teacher of the learning disabled, wanted her graduating students to find jobs. Max Winthrop, CEO and owner of Winthrop's department stores, refused to hire her students until Kiley became part of the deal. She quickly discovered that Winthrop's policy of "satisfaction guaranteed" only began to describe what Max offered....

#302 THE COWBOY Jayne Ann Krentz (Ladies and Legends, Book 3)

Sexy cowboys in pin-striped suits were writer Margaret Lark's idea of romantic heroes. Rafe Cassidy seemed to fit the picture, but he had seriously compromised his credibility once before. He'd ordered Margaret out of his life for being loyal to her boss rather than to her lover. Now he was determined to get her back—to prove his honor was safe.

#303 ONLY YESTERDAY Karen Toller Whittenburg

Merry McLennan, former "little" Miss Sunshine and child model, thought she had buried her old identity for good. She never wanted to be used again for her looks or put on display. Until she met Lee Zurbaron, a psychologist whose latest research project dealt with child stars. Once again Merry found herself in the spotlight... just where she didn't want to be.

#304 REMEMBRANCE Lynn Michaels EDITOR'S CHOICE

When Cathy Martin returned to her grandmother's home in Martha's Vineyard to coauthor the actress's memoirs, she hadn't expected to meet her grandfather's ghost. Was *he* haunting the house—or was it Fin McGraw, his look-alike? Fin was definitely flesh and blood—and eager to help Cathy explore all the bumps and noises that happen in the night....